THE
WHY
FILES

MARSHALL MILLER

BLUE FORGE PRESS
Port Orchard, Washington

Blue Forge Press is the print division of the volunteer-run, federal 501(c)3 nonprofit company, Blue Forge Group, founded in 1989 and dedicated to bringing light to the shadows and voice to the silence. We strive to empower storytellers across all walks of life with our four divisions: Blue Forge Press, Blue Forge Films, Blue Forge Gaming, and Blue Forge Records. Find out more at www.BlueForgeGroup.Com

Blue Forge Press
7419 Ebbert Drive Southeast
Port Orchard, Washington 98367
blueforgepress@gmail.com
360-550-2071 ph.txt

MORE BY THE AUTHOR

SPECIAL AGENT KIM KUPAR NOVELS

Jade Eyes
They

THE TSCHAAA INFESTATION

Book 1: The Gathering Storm
Book 2: The Tsunami
Book 3: Typhoon of Steel
Free Range Protocol: Tales of the Tschaaa
Beyond the Great Compromise: Tales of the Tschaaa
Survivors: Escaping the Tschaaa

ANTHOLOGIES

Monstrosity (Unnerving Anthology)
Descent (Unnerving Anthology)
Wicked (Unnerving Anthology)
The Mighty Pen
Unconditional
Cascadia
Tales of the Slug
Super: Unexpected Heroes Arise

COLLECTED WORKS & MORE

Inhumanity: A Year of Stories
The Island (The Haunting of Orchard House)
Shane (Angels of Anarchy)

Dedication

The following series of stories is dedicated to all the LEOs, First Responders, and military personnel who help to keep this great country in one piece. All of us know that truth is often stranger than fiction. Stay frosty.

Acknowledgments

Thanks again to the Blue Forge Press staff and the DiMarco Clan for making this book possible.

TABLE OF CONTENTS

THE
WHY
FILES

MARSHALL MILLER

FILE 1
IT BEGINS

Richard Johnson stood in the remains of the isolated and illegal cabin hidden in the Olympic National Forest. The shards of glass under his feet were thick and so deep red they appeared black and it took the special agent a few moments to realize it was blackened blood, not the natural color of the glass.

The special agent had been sent up to the Port Angeles area from his assigned position at the Office of the Special Agent in Charge, Homeland Security Investigations in Seattle. A small smile crossed Richard's face as he thought of the reason behind his being sent up to this forest. On his desk was framed copy of a photocopy of a famous poster. It read *I Want to Believe* and sported a supposed photo of a UFO on it. From day one in the office, Richard was an agent who became known as an investigator attracted to investigations involving the odd and weird. So, when the small two-person Resident Agent Office asked for assistance, Brad Ball, the Deputy Special Agent in Charge, sent Richard. It got him out of the office, so he didn't see it as a punishment.

Senior Agent Raquel Burke and Special Agent Sam Morris had met him at the entrance to the National Forest Service access road. The road was more of a trail than a real road, so Richard had been glad he was driving his four-wheel-drive SUV. During the unusually hot summer, the grass and vegetation were high and dry in the forest. He knew he would have to be mindful of the fire danger.

"Glad you could make it, Richard," Raquel said as she shook his hand. He had first met the zaftig brunette when Richard was with the U.S. Border Patrol in the Yuma, Arizona Sector. Raquel had actually helped him transition to a Special Agent/Criminal Investigator with Homeland Security after he aided her in a human trafficking case in San Luis. Now, she was the Senior Agent/Supervisor in the small two-person Port Angeles Office. Anything on the northern part of Kitsap Peninsula, when it came to investigations and enforcement, Raquel and Sam had to handle. And just as this odd call had come in, the two special agents were already involved in a significant smuggling investigation from Victoria Island, Canada. As it was, they were glad to see Richard.

"Glad I can be of help, Raquel. Gets me out of the office."

"Up this road," the woman pointed as she spoke, "you'll find Senior Special Agent Tom Olafson of the National Forest Service. He has a couple of sheriff's deputies from the Drug Task Force with him. They're waiting on a local tracker and his dogs to search the area."

Richard frowned. All this for a reported small marijuana grow operation in a state where marijuana was now legal to possess and sell as long as you had a license?

"By the frown, I can tell you are confused why we asked for help," said the senior agent. "Well, I'll let Tom explain after you see the crime scene. It will be easier."

"Crime scene?" asked Richard.

"Lots of blood and destruction," answered Sam Morris. "But, no bodies. Killing and disappearing people over a small pot field makes no sense."

"Especially when Washington State legalized it," said Richard. "And the DEA and everyone else is looking the other way, as long it does not cross the Canadian border."

"Okay, Raquel. I've got it. You two have fun finishing your other case. I heard it's a doozy."

"Chinese Triad and all," Raquel answered. "Thanks again. I'm glad they sent you. It's like old times."

"Yep. You can buy me a beer before I leave the area. I'll probably be here a couple of days."

"It's a date," the senior agent said. Then she and Sam climbed into their vehicle and drove away.

As Richard slowly drove up the unfamiliar trail, he could see the recent tire tracks and crushed vegetation which marked the path of the other law enforcement vehicles. He also saw how dry the undergrowth was around the large fir trees. The forest was a tinderbox. Over a mile up the pathway through more overgrown brush Richard saw the rear ends of two SUVs, one with government plates. *This must be the place,* thought the special agent. He pulled over to the side of the trail as best he could and exited his vehicle. He tried to see the cabin mentioned in the report but could not. Whoever had built it had picked a perfect concealment spot.

Richard started to call out when a massive man in a police tactical vest stepped out from the brush.

"You must be Richard Johnson," the man said. "I'm Special Agent Tom Olafson. Pleased to meet you."

Olafson's oversized hand engulfed Richard's in the handshake. Richard was not small and had a stocky build, but this Forest Service agent made him feel small. He was beginning to get used to the large Nordic types whose ancestors had settled in towns like Poulsbo and then spread out. Richard thought they built large Texans and Arizonans, but when the special agent moved up here, he had to re-evaluate what "large" meant after meeting the local residents.

"Pleased to meet you, sir. Looks like someone picked a good place to hide."

"You haven't seen the half of it," Olafson said with a wide grin. "Follow me and I'll show you the rest."

It took some five minutes of walking down a pathway with concealed handrails to reach the cabin. When Richard saw it, he whistled.

"Someone had some military camouflage experience," he said. "They also spent some money on all that netting. How'd it get noticed?"

"One of our seasonal fire watch people saw smoke and sounded the alarm. Everyone responded and they found this."

"I understand there was some evidence of a possible assault or violence?" Richard asked.

The modern-day version of Eric the Red laughed. "After I show you the interior of this building, you'll see that is the understatement of the year."

Next, Richard was staring at the broken colored and bloodstained glass on the white tile floor. Or what had once been an actual and complete floor. Now in the center of the main room was a massive hole. As Richard looked up from the hole, he could see a matching penetration which took out what had been the back wall.

"No signs of an explosion, like with a Meth lab?" Richard asked.

"No, sir. If you look closely, you'll see the back wall looks like it was pulled out. The floor looks like something dug underneath it and pulled it down into the hole. Which, by the way, is connected to a collapsed tunnel."

Richard stood and surveyed the entire scene before he spoke again. "Seen any mutated mountain beavers the size of a Mack truck around?"

Tom laughed. "I already thought of that. Even a full-grown male grizzly would have trouble doing this. And they don't usually dig tunnels."

"So, Tom, I guess we assume it is human-caused."

The tall modern Viking shrugged his shoulders. "Your guess is as good as mine. We do have one more oddity that may mean something." Olafson turned and yelled out at the two sheriff detectives from the drug task force. In a few moments, one brought a large paper bag used to hold evidence. Tom took the bag and gingerly reached in with his gloved hands. Slowly the man pulled a two foot long, three inches in diameter object from the container.

"Have you ever seen anything like this?" the forest service special agent commented as he held it up for Richard to see.

Richard froze. He had seen something like this years before, as a young twelve-year-old boy. Before Olafson noticed his reaction, Richard said, "I may have someone I can call who may help."

"Good," replied the Forest Service agent. "This thing reminds me of the plant they call the Devils Club. But these protrusions on this thing are more like hairs than thorns or stickers on plants like that. This looks more animal-like to me."

"You going to send it to the state laboratory?" asked Richard as he tried not to stare at the solid stick-like object which was all too familiar.

"Eventually. I'll hold on to it until this cabin had been thoroughly searched and everything processed." Olafson glance at his watch. "Dan and his tracking dogs should be here any minute."

"Dogs?"

"Yes, Richard. Some of the blood we found tests as human. Someone may have crawled off to die, whatever caused their wounds."

"Let me try a find a higher spot where I can get a cellphone signal," said Richard. "Then I'll see if my contact can help."

"Okay. Up that incline is a large old growth stump.

That may help."

Five minutes of a slight climb and Richard clambered up a six-foot-high stump. There he obtained a couple of cell connection bars on his phone. He hit the speed dial. A minute later, a familiar voice answered.

"Johnson residence."

"Dad, it's Richard."

"Richard! Hey, Son, where ya at? Your mother's wondering when you are coming to Port Orchard for a visit."

Richard smiled. All mothers were the same. They wanted their children back in the nest no matter how old they were.

"Well, Dad, I'm actually on your side of the Sound. But this call is business."

"Business?" the retired Border Patrol agent asked. His father, Mike, had been the reason for Richard's interest in Law Enforcement and his own stint in the Border Patrol before becoming a special agent. So, Richard knew his dad's old patrol instincts were questioning why his son called now.

"Yes, Dad." Richard took a breath, then let it out. "Remember when I told you as I was leaving to go to basic training in the Air Force? About something I had found that belonged to Grandpa?"

There was silence on the other end of the line. Richard remembered the look his father had given him when he mentioned what he had found snooping all those years ago.

"Forget you saw that, Richard," Mike Johnson had said in a gruff voice. "Your Grandpa took something he wasn't supposed to. Mention it to anyone and there will be hell to pay."

Richard had managed to get a guarantee of an explanation when he was back from training. One thing led to another and Richard never received the answer. Now, the time for a response was being forced onto everyone.

"You found something," his dad said.

"Yes, Dad. Can you meet me at the parking area on the west end of the Hood Canal Bridge?"

"It will take a while, but yes."

"Good. Call me on my cell phone when you hit the bridge."

"Okay, Son. See you there."

Richard made his way back to the wrecked cabin just when Dan and his dogs arrived.

"Got through?" asked Tom.

"Yes, sir. And I see your tracking dogs are here."

The dogs were two traditional bloodhound types, paired with a large Pitbull mix. Richard asked Dan Smith, the scruffy born dog handler, why the combination of breeds.

"The two hounds have the noses to do the tracking. Bruno here," Dan jabbed a thumb at the Pitbull, "he'll take on anything. Saw him face down a bull elk during rutting season. Damned elk will take on wolves when they are in a rut. Bruno slammed into the bull elk, sent him running. Had a hell of a time getting Bruno to come back."

"How about a grizzly bear?" asked Richard.

"How about a T-rex?"

That had elicited some laughter from the law enforcement types as Dan set his dogs to work. However, an odd thing happened when Dan tried to get his bloodhounds near the oversized hole in the cabin's living area. The two dogs refused to cross the threshold. Dan cursed, pushed, prodded and was knocked over for his efforts. Bruno began to howl and bark as he stood his ground. But he would not cross the cabin threshold, either.

"Something... *bad* was here," said Tom.

"I'm going to meet that contact I mentioned in a couple of hours," said Richard. "I'll show him my cell phone photo of it."

"Hope you or the lab can come up with some answers," replied Tom. "Someone was running a small grow operation to raise and sell some nontaxable marijuana, among other things, just like moonshiners did post Prohibition. And that blood we found says they are now dead." He looked at Richard.

"I don't like people or animals fucking around in my forest."

Some two hours later, Richard sat in the parking and tourist overlook area on the west end of the Hood Canal Bridge. In addition to the size and flora of the Hood Canal area, occasionally people could see orca pods swim near. The Hood Canal floating bridge would occasionally open to allow Trident submarines and other sea craft through. Today, there were a couple of parked cars with tourist types out with cameras.

Richard recognized his father's Grand Cherokee SUV approaching and flashed his lights. Mike Johnson saw and pulled his vehicle driver's side to driver's side with the window rolled down.

"Brought you some coffee, Son. My own brew."

"Thanks, Dad." Richard took the proffered coffee and sipped at it. It was still warm from the high-end thermos used for transport. As he used the coffee as an excuse not to start talking about the sensitive subject, he examined his father. Mike was slender and still fit from working outdoors despite his graying hair. Richard took after his mother's family, so he was thicker and broader of the chest. People did say that on the telephone, he and his Dad sounded exactly alike.

"Well, Son, you said you needed to talk and not on the telephone. So, like they used to say, it's your dime."

Richard handed his father his cell phone with the displayed picture of the object. The elder Johnson stared at the cellphone display for several minutes before giving it back, as if to decide what he was going to say about it.

Finally, he spoke. "I never thought I'd have to deal with that... thing ever again. Not after the effect it had on Grandpa."

Richard waited for his father to continue. A good investigator knew when it was best to be patient and let people talk when they wanted to and not interrupt. You learned more from listening.

Mike Johnson took a sip of his coffee, then began to explain. "Your Grandpa, my Dad, was an eighteen-year-old private who had been in Korea one week when the Communists came across the border. He was there when the North Koreans pushed all the U.S. Forces back to the Pusan

Perimeter. September 1950, MacArthur pulled off the Inchon Landing and Grandpa was part of the push back up into North Korea. They made him a Sergeant one day, he was shot and wounded the next."

"So that is how you got his Purple Heart," said Richard.

"Yep. Grandpa didn't talk about it much. A grateful nation sent him stateside to serve out his remaining time. He asked to be sent someplace warm, so he was sent to Nevada, soon to be the Nevada Test Sites where a lot of nukes were tested. He met Grandma in Nevada and they were married. She was pregnant with me soon after that and Grandpa told the Army he'd re-enlist if he could stay in Nevada. They said great, so he was in place to become one of the Atomic Soldiers. That's how he came into contact with that thing you found hidden in his chest of drawers."

Mike paused for a moment as he sipped his coffee, then continued. "One of the early highly classified tests was underground with a new H-bomb design. It blew a nice big hole in the ground. It also opened a hole to… well, *Elsewhere* is what Grandpa called it. Son, remember that science fiction movie made around 1954 about the giant ants?"

"Sure, Dad. They still were showing it on TV all the time when I was growing up. What does that have to do with Grandpa and this object?"

"That movie was based on leaked classified information. None of it happened in the sewers and drains of Los Angeles, but the ants… they happened in Nevada. Only they were not Earth ants."

Richard stared at his father for a few moments. "Dad, now you have me completely confused. I knew when I mentioned what I had seen hidden in Grandpa's sock drawers it upset you and you didn't want to talk about it, but this is bizarre. What looked like a mummified piece of plant...?"

"Not plant," Mike interrupted. "Ant."

"Alright. If you say so. So, something nasty must have happened for you and Grandpa to hide it from the rest of the family."

"I'm getting to that, Son. It took years for Grandpa to tell me this after a few drinks. Please bear with me."

Richard nodded yes, and his father continued.

"Grandpa was an E-5 by then, had a squad of men assigned to him. They were sent out with full weapons and gear plus some Geiger counters when there was a report of someone running around the area of that classified test. The soldiers found a tunnel that shouldn't have been there. Out of the tunnel came these ants, two to three yards long. Grandpa and his troops shot first and asked questions later. A couple of the ants chomped on the soldiers, killed three of them when the tunnel collapsed due to the weapons fire. After the Army realized Grandpa was not drunk or crazy, they sent out a full company with two light tanks followed by an engineer platoon. They mopped up the remaining ants, loaded up a couple carcasses for study and blew the tunnel to bits. Then, the engineers covered the area with cement, reportedly rigged up some boobytraps to let the Army know if the giant ants came back."

"Did they come back?" Richard asked.

His father shrugged. "Grandpa never knew. He was retired on full disability and a nondisclosure form to keep him quiet. After he heard some brainiacs say they were not Earth ants, but just a creature that looked like ants and filled the same niche, he got the hell out of Dodge. They had animal-type lungs, but their carapace was different so they could grow to a large size. They make those huge coconut crabs in the Pacific look small."

"But Grandpa stole a piece of one. Why?"

"To prove to himself that it was not some nightmare or that he was nuts. I was born in 1954 when that movie was made. When I started watching that movie on TV years later, Grandpa pulled me aside, swore me to secrecy, and showed me the piece of giant ant antenna he got away with. He said he had to tell someone, and thought he could trust his oldest son."

"And now I have really stumbled into it," said Richard.

"Son, I'm asking you to find a way to keep Grandpa and me out of this. Years ago, when I was in the Border Patrol on the Southwest Border, I did some snooping around. Someone must have seen my name, connected it to Grandpa. One day on patrol out in the desert I received a visit by two black-suited men in a black SUV. I was told to stop snooping. I did. It's easy to get rid of a body in the desert."

Richard knew he was between a rock and a hard place. If he didn't pass on this information that he had just received, people could be hurt or killed. But if he did, his Dad could wind up in prison. He'd have to figure something out before things went from bad to worse.

"Well, Dad, the sample the State and Locals found is being sent to the State Patrol Lab. Maybe the results will come back fast enough so I won't have to mention any of this."

"Hope so, Son. But if it's between a bunch of innocents being hurt or killed and me, well..."

"We'll cross that bridge when we get to it. However, it sounds as if the Multiverse theory was just proven."

The elder Johnson left with the promise from Richard to stop by whenever he made his way back to Seattle. Richard drove back to Port Angeles, stopping at the local gun and surplus store. He picked up some full metal jacket nine-millimeter rounds for his pistol and the MP-5 in his trunk. The special agent also picked up a small five shell box of Sabot Slugs for his twelve-gauge pump. He was a firearms instructor for Homeland Security, so no one looked askance at him carrying extra weapons and ammunition. Then Richard drove to the Forest Service HQ Office.

When he met Agent Olafson, Richard discovered the situation had changed. There was a witness. A young twelve-year-old Mexican boy had been picked up wearing some bloody clothes. Richard went to the interview room where he was being held. His Border Patrol Spanish might come in handy.

The Forest Service agents had gotten the young boy some extra clothes and some hamburgers with a milkshake. The kid was eating as if he had not had a decent meal in days, which could have been the truth. Drug dealers were notorious for being cheap bastards unless you were family.

"Hola, Jefe," Richard greeted the young boy. *"¿Habla ingles?"*

"Yes. I was born here," the boy answered.

"Okay. I'm Homeland Security Special Agent Johnson. What's your name?"

"Jesus Durango."

"Okay, Jesus. The other officers told me you were there in the *bosque,* the forest. Can you tell me what happened?"

The boy looked at him with eyes older than the twelve-year-old body containing them. "My Uncle Marcos, he's dead, isn't he?"

"We don't know, Jesus. Why do you think he is dead?"

The young Mexican-American boy looked down and began to shake. The female Sheriff's deputy who was sitting near him gently touch his arm.

"It's okay, Jesus. You're safe here."

"Lady, you didn't see the *hormigas.*"

"Ants," Richard interrupted. "You saw ants, right?"

Jesus looked up at Richard. The boy's eyes bespoke of a remembered terror.

"The ants. They looked like big ants. They came up through the floor. Uncle Marcos fell into the hole and screamed." Tears streamed down the boy's cheeks. "Mateo shot at them until one smashed through the wall and bit him. Mateo's blood spurt all over me. I ran."

Jesus began to sob and buried his face in the arms of the female deputy. Richard stood up and walked out of the interview room. Tom Olafson was waiting for him.

"He started babbling about the 'hormigas' when we found him along an old logging road near the cabin," said the large man. "Jesus was covered with blood. I'm sending his clothes to the lab."

Richard paused in thought for a moment. Then he spoke. "You believe him? About giant ant-looking creatures?"

"No. But something or someone hacked up the Uncle and Mateo," replied Tom. "And it was not the boy."

Richard looked back thru the two-way mirror at Jesus in the interview room. The boy was still sobbing. At that moment, Richard made a decision.

"Come on, Tom. Let me buy you coffee while I tell you a story."

The two agents sat at a back table in the local diner. Tom was cursing under his breath.

"Just what in the hell am I supposed to do with this story?" the agent asked. "Richard, if I walk in and tell anyone up the chain, well, first they will send me to pee in a bottle for drugs. Then, they'll send me to a shrink if they don't just lock me up."

"I know it's hard to believe, Tom..."

"Hard? It's impossible, Richard."

The two law enforcement officers sat quietly, staring into their coffee cups. Tom broke the silence. "So, if I rush it, the specimen I send to the lab could be turned around in a couple days."

"The problem with that," interjected Richard, "is they will see it is animal, or insect, whatever those things test as in our part of the universe—then they will argue because it does not match anything they know of in this area. Then they will claim the sample was contaminated. Then they will have someone else run tests…"

"I know, Richard. It will turn into a complete goat rope. Days later, we are back to square one." The large man motioned to the waitress for a refill. "By that time, maybe more dead."

"But no one believes us without more proof," said Richard. "It's too much like a bad Saturday afternoon creature-feature."

"So, we are stewed, screwed, and tattooed," replied Tom.

The two men silently sat as they drank their refreshed cups of coffee. Richard broke the silence. "How far do we take this?"

"You want to do something if it has to be unofficial, off the record?" replied the agent.

"If it means stopping people from being killed, yes."

Tom slurped his coffee down, then stood up. "Come on. I'll pay."

Tom paid and left a substantial tip. The two special agents walked out to the parking area as Tom put a hunk of chewing tobacco in his mouth.

"Bad habit but better than smoking I guess."

"One habit I never took up," said Richard.

"Don't. It's expensive and your wife will hate it." Tom stopped by the Forest Service SUV and looked around. "Well, no one in the parking lot. So, like I asked, how far do you want to take this, like, now?"

"First, that female sheriff's deputy who was there—" Richard began to ask.

Tom interrupted, "Julie's okay. I asked her to wait until I turned in my report before she does hers."

"Let's do it then, Tom. If we wait for officialdom to act, it may be weeks, months. So far, all we have is two missing dopers and a hysterical twelve-year-old. Can you imagine if all that happened at a campground?"

"That is my nightmare. So, Richard, I have a few friends not affiliated with the Forest Service. They will help me do most anything if I say it is to protect the Port Angeles area. I can call them, and they will come with some artillery. Interested?"

Richard's face broke into a broad grin. "Hell, yeah. I know my Grandpa would have been."

"Okay," replied Tom. "I'll need to make some phone calls. I'll call you at your motel room."

"Good," said Richard. The two men shook hands.

"It begins, Richard," said Tom ominously. "Other than my stint in the Army, some time being shot at overseas, I have lived my whole life here." He shook his head. "I don't like anybody or anything fucking with my forest."

Tom did fast work, as the next morning at O-Dark-Thirty, he met Richard in the hotel parking lot. With him were two other fair-haired men, almost as large as Tom and sporting woodland camouflaged fatigues.

"Richard, these are two of my Army buddies, Jack

Swanson and Matt Anderson. They're my lifetime hunting partners also."

Richard shook hands with the two men as Tom said, "We have one more coming."

"Who's that?" Richard asked.

"Dan Smith. He said he has a tracking dog that will fit the bill this time."

As they waited for Dan, Richard took a look at some non-official "artillery" they brought. Tom had a large, powerful .388 Lapua rifle constructed on a beefed AR-15 frame.

"Jack here did it," Tom said. "He's a gunsmith by trade now. I have some home loads for long range shooting competition that should do the trick. Ballistics are just this side of .50 caliber HMG rounds." Tom then pulled a stubby-looking weapon with an oversized diameter barrel.

"This is assigned to my office. It's a surplus M-79 grenade launcher. We put together a couple of black powder flash-bang shells. I also scrounged a smoke round and we made a flechette rounds for close in work."

"I have my MP-5 and a twelve gauge with sabot slugs," said Richard. "I hope I don't have to use them."

"Well, we all hope that," answered Tom. "Jack has his own designed magazine fed twelve gauge and Matt has an M1-A1 in .308. We a so all have sidearms, so we are well healed I would dare say."

As they talked, a beat-up four-wheel drive van drove up and parked. Dan Smith, the driver, stepped out with a huge doubled-barreled weapon.

"What do you have there, Dan?" asked Jack.

"A 500 Nito Express. An old-timey elephant gun. I found it at an auction."

As Dan spoke, two canines walked around the back of the van. Richard saw one was Bruno, the Pitbull mix from the day before. Walking next to it was a Dachshund.

"Is that a wiener dog?" asked Matt.

"Hey, it's a Dachshund, a badger hound. Insult Hans enough, and he may bite you."

All the men laughed at the thought of the low-slung dog running around and ankle-biting them.

"I hear they are nasty," said Richard.

"They're bred to go down the burrows of badgers, bite their asses," replied Dan. "So, like an old Army tunnel rat, they have a tendency to be on edge."

"Well, the things we may run into will be bigger that badgers," said Tom.

"That's why Bruno is here. Out of pure dog pride, Bruno will not let Hans go someplace where he can also fit. Letting the small dog show him up will make his balls shrink." The five men all laughed, then went to their respective vehicles.

A half hour of driving, then five minutes of walking and the five men were at the wrecked cabin. Nothing had been disturbed, which told them the cause of the destruction had not returned. Jack whistled as he examined the hole in the cabin floor.

"Man, all I can think of is a prehistoric mountain beaver," said the local man. "I read they were as big as bears."

"Well, sir, to be honest," said Richard. "What we are looking for maybe a lot larger. And nasty."

"Big as an elephant?" Asked Dan.

"Maybe," Richard replied. "When you see what I think we will find, all I can say is shoot first and ask questions later. I don't want to tell you more in case we find nothing. If certain people find out you know too much, it might get sticky."

The other men all shrugged.

"We're all former military," said Matt. "We understand keeping your mouth shut about stuff you're not supposed to know. So, like in Shakespeare, lay on McDuff." Richard looked at Tom. The modern-day Eric the Red grinned, then spoke.

"Alright. So, how about we climb this rise here and then down the other side. I bet you there's an opening about the size of this tunnel."

"Like you said," answered Richard, "It's your forest."

The five men and two dogs made good time, Dan helping Hans keep up because of the Dachshund's short legs. As predicted, there was a matching hole opposite of the cabin's location. Richard had brought a couple of road flares to use as torches if necessary, but the other four men produced headband mounted small flashlights. They gave enough light to see as they slowly entered the tunnel opening.

"Stay frosty," Richard said.

"Frosty as last year's bad winter," answered Tom. The two canines began to growl as they caught the scent of something they did not like. Hans took off like a shot on his short legs, surprising the men. Dan cursed under his breath as he brought his heavy elephant gun up to port arms.

"Damn dog. Does this all the time…"

Hans let out a howl that was cut off in mid sound. Bruno let out a hunting snarl and surged ahead.

"Guns up!" Tom called out as the five men all began to jog ahead into the partially lit cavern. The floor of the tunnel began to slope downward as they tried to catch up with Bruno. Then a fighting bay and snarl came from around the corner in a sudden bend of the tunnel. Tom was first around the corner and let out a yell of surprise as a strange trilling sound washed down the walls of the underground network.

Illuminated by the headlamps of the other four men was an… Ant. But not a regular ant, not even one blown up to bull elk size. Richard saw not the smooth chitinous hair-covered exoskeleton of an Earth insect, but rather a six-legged body covered with smaller interlocking segmented plates much like the armor of a Japanese Samurai.

The Ant-Creature was holding the two dogs down with its front legs as it seemed to be looking at the new arrivals with it two large compound eyes. The special agent had no additional time to examine the creature as the discharge of Dan's elephant gun shook the entire area. The oversized shell smashed the Ant between its two main eyes and some odd copper colored liquid spurted out from the bullet entrance hole. The beast seemed to stagger, then collapsed sideways and partially curled its body. The two dogs did not move from the floor of the cavern. Dan cursed and scrambled forward.

"Hans! Bruno!" yelled Dan. The other four men formed a protective perimeter around Dan and his dogs. Richard took the side closest to the Ant so he could examine it with his tactical flashlight. A closer look revealed the details of the segmented body plates which seemed quite flexible. They were so much like Samurai armor that Richard expected to see a "Made in Japan" notice on the body. Also, the clawed feet also had opposable tentacles above the claws, almost like elongated thumbs.

"I think the dogs are still alive," Dan called out. "Just stunned."

"Shall we act like sheep and get the flock out of here?" asked Tom. "Take a photo with your cellphone. We've found what we expected, Richard."

"How are we going to close this down, Tom?" Richard asked. "You know there has to be…"

A second Ant was on top of them almost before they noticed. Jack's semi-auto magazine fed twelve gauge exploded into action as he was the closest to the new arrival. Three quick slug rounds and the creature collapsed, its destroyed head just inches from Jack's feet.

"Move!" Tom called out, and everyone moved. Richard grabbed up Hans under his left arm, so his right was free to use the strapped and slung MP-5. Dan was trying to hang Bruno around his shoulder when a third beast came trilling up on them. Richard sprayed the Ant with nine-millimeter rounds. The creature automatically turned towards the source of the sharp objects striking it as a loud boom echoed differently than the elephant gun. Tom's .338 Lapua rifle blew a good-sized hole in what was on an insect the thorax. The Ant twisted, slashed its jaws at Tom who managed to jump just out of range. Richard jammed his MP-5 towards the back of the odd head and fired a burst from close range. That did the trick and the Ant collapsed to the dirt floor in a heap. Everyone began to scramble back the way they came.

"What the fuck is this?" Matt called out.

"A lousy movie!" Jack called back. Matt's M1-A1 spoke as another Ant came from the same direction as the last.

"Goddamn connecting tunnels," Matt cursed as he fired at two Ants at once.

Tom fired his rifle again, then again and again. "Reloading!" Tom cried out as he put a fresh four round magazine in the weapon.

Richard looked ahead in time to see part of the tunnel begin to collapse as an Ant head tried to force its way in. He fired the rest of his magazine, then let Hans slide to the tunnel floor as he reloaded with the spare magazine clipped side to side with the now empty one. He fired a dozen rounds in a pattern on the thrusting head which could be covered with a silver half dollar. The Ant collapsed. Richard put the MP-5 on safe and slung it to his back as he swapped it with his twelve-gauge pump shotgun. He was about to pick up Hans again when Tom beat him to it. The big man slung the Dachshund on the back of his neck like a fur stole.

"Let's go," Tom said.

Everyone began to run.

The sun's early morning light was illuminating the tops

of the fir trees as the five men reached the tunnel entrance. Bruno was beginning to come around, as was Hans. Dan mumbled words of encouragement as he ministered to his dog family. The others formed a circle of security around Dan and his two dogs.

"What the fuck was those things?" Jack asked.

"Ant creatures from another reality or universe," replied Richard.

"Well, we have physical evidence of what happened at the cabin," Tom interjected. "The question now is what are we going to do with it? We're going to need a small army to deal with…"

Tom was unable to finish his comment as a substantial something came crashing through the forest. Seconds later an even larger Ant than the ones in the identified tunnel nest came bursting into the small clearing. Richard was closest, so he pumped three sabot slugs into its head as fast as he could pump his shotgun. The Ant collapsed in a massive heap. There was silence for a few moments as everyone examined the dead insect-like a monster.

"Segmented armor like a Samurai or Roman Legionnaire," Richard pointed out. "I bet you the internal organs are a bit different. Whatever planet they developed on, I bet you there is some kind of lungs in that thing. Different evolution so they could grow larger yet have sufficient oxygen to function.

"You seem to know a lot about these horrors," Max stated.

"Family   history,"   answered   Richard.   "I'll

explain later..."

There was suddenly loud trilling nearby, then more Ants like the one they had just killed forced their way through the forest.

"Fuck!" yelled Tom as he began to fire.

"Damned Warrior Ants!" Richard called out. "They circled around us."

"Shoot them in their goddammed big brains," Jack yelled out as he emptied his shotgun and then reloaded a fresh magazine. Matt took another Ant-Creature down with his rifle when he was bowled over by a smaller one that came rushing out from the cavern. The man screamed as the mandibles crushed and slashed his right leg. Richard emptied his shotgun into the beast and it collapsed on top of its victim.

"Fire in the hole!" yelled Tom Olafson as he used the M-79 to fire a flashbang round back into the tunnel opening. The fighting men made sure not to be looking into the cavern as the explosive round detonated. Pieces of the tunnel ceiling fell down as some odd vibrating non-human cries came from further down inside the hill.

"Time to haul ass!" Tom called out as he reloaded his rifle. Richard helped Matt use his rifle sling to create a tourniquet on the damaged leg. Then the larger Jack boosted him up and across his shoulders in a fireman's carry. Richard slung his weapons and picked up Matts M1-A1.

"There's a game trail downslope," said Dan as he herded the now two mobile canines forward. Somehow, he had managed to hang onto his elephant gun. The human fighting group tried to work their way through the thick brush and not trip.

"Your flashbang round seemed to slow them up," Richard said to Tom as they thread their way through the underbrush.

"I did some study also," Tom answered. "Ants hate any kind of fire near their nest, will throw their bodies on it to keep it from spreading."

"Here's the trail!" Dan called out. Then his dogs began to bark and snarl. The other man soon saw why as several more Ants were using the trail to carry objects back to their nest in their oversized mandibles.

"Foragers," Richard called out. He used Matt's rifle to shoot the two nearest creatures, which collapsed with their loads. The weapon clicked on an empty chamber and the agent dropped it. Richard reached back into his pack, grabbing a road flare. An ear-numbing report of a gun told Richard that Dan had managed to bring his elephant gun back into play. Tom saw the road flare in his hand.

"That may start a hell of a forest fire," the forest agent said.

"Not if the Ants put it out with their bodies which should give us time to flee."

Richard used the igniter cap to light the flare and let it burn bright for a few moments. He then threw it just to the right of the remaining giant insects. One look at the bright flame, which soon set a bush on fire, and the remaining Ant-Creatures dropped their loads of foraged food and began to bite and claw at the evil fire.

"Let's move!" Richard yelled as he picked up Matt's

rifle and made a dash around the ass ends of the Ants. The creatures from another reality acted enough like Earth insects that they were focused entirely on the spreading flames and ignored the humans. Down the forest trail, the men and dogs scrambled. Richard glance back and saw the smoke was no longer as thick.

"Those Ants are putting out the fire, sacrificing themselves for their nest," said Richard.

"Someone from our fire watch will see the smoke and investigate," said Tom. "So, we'll have a ride."

"Those damned things had elk carcasses in their mouths." Jack humped wounded Matt down the trail.

"I guess the hunters are going to be pissed this year," replied Tom.

The sounds of helicopter blades beating the air into submission made the group lookup.

"That was quick," stated Richard.

"Those aren't ours," said Tom.

All black helicopters came zipping in at low altitude. As soon as they began to hover, armed tactical personnel fast-roped into the forest. Fully automatic weapons fire echoed from the area of the flaring fire as more and more troops were inserted in the woods.

"Someone was tipped off about us."

"I guess your friend Julie decided to do her report early," replied Richard. "Now the fun with the Men in Black begins."

Three hours later, Richard was sitting in the back of a blacked-out government version of a tour bus. He was drinking a cup of coffee after being grilled by a Man in Black with the name, of course, of Agent Smith. Richard assumed there were several Smiths and maybe even some Jones from an unknown alphabet agency raking his comrades over the coals. Richard kept his father out of the conversation, but of course, Richard figured the senior Johnson would get a visit just to remind him to keep quiet. Richard had signed a couple of Non-Disclosure Upon Pain of Disappearing Forms. He chuckled. At least all this meant that Richard's Report of Investigation would be short and sweet.

Agent Smith came into the room with a secured communication satellite phone.

"Your boss," was all the dead-eyed man said. Richard took the telephone and answered, "Johnson here... Yes, sir. I understand. Reports have been written for my signature... I'll head back tomorrow... Yes, I'm fine... See you soon."

Agent Smith took the SAT phone back and said, "You're free to go," then walked him to a rear door in the bus. His G-Ride was parked a few feet away. A quick check showed all his equipment was neatly placed in it. Richard laughed, got in, fastened his seat belt and started the SUV. He drove to the local diner where he and Tom had made the first plans. At a back table was Tom. Richard walked up, shook his hand and sat down.

"So, now what, Richard?" Tom asked.

"You still have a small Mom and Pop Store that sells

DVDs and videos around here?"

"Yep. What are you looking for, Richard?"

"A classic. *Them!* I figured to watch it in my motel room with some beer and pizza. Want to join me?"

Tom began to laugh. "Hell, why not? We can be great movie critics."

Richard motioned to the waitress for the check.

Kim Kupar jerked awake. It had been a while since she had 'The Dream.' She referred to it as The Dream as it was unique, memorable and based on an actual event. The huge feline starring in her face, the jade eyes of the modified Bengal tiger just inches from her face. Kim thought she was about to be Sir Khan's next victim when he disappeared like a ghost. And, he was still missing.

Once a Bengal tiger, then a feline of very mixed parentage, the human-modified creature was to be her killer. John Wang, Kim's lover and betrayer, created the sabretooth cat as a potential item for sale in his smuggling and criminal empire, then used as an assassination method. Instead, Sir Khan killed John and let Kim live. The special agent knew the fallout from the investigation could have cost her job. Her partner Rex Moyer's actions and testimony and the saving of human trafficking victims led to Homeland Security Investigation to reconsider her worth as a federal investigator.

The special agent knew why she had The Dream. Her supervisors at the Homeland Security Investigations in Seattle had told her to be in the office bright and early for a new primary partner and a new assignment. The one hint was that it involved looking for Sir Khan and other anomalies. She and the big cat seemed joined at the hip.

The Argentine and Punjabi raven-haired woman rolled over in her townhouse bed, tried to find a new comfortable spot. She needed to be rested, dammit. She closed her own jade eyes and willed herself to sleep.

Richard Johnson made his coffee strong that morning. His night was filled with nightmarish images of creatures that were horribly real, although few would believe it. Giant ant creatures from some other reality had intruded into first his Grandfather's and then his life. But the Men in Black had told him and others that to discuss these creatures would result in people being locked up in mental institutions to protect the secret. So, the Homeland Security Senior Agent was left with a couple of hidden photographs and the occasional nightmare.

Now it seemed that the incident and his ability to keep his mouth shut resulted in Assistant Special Agent in Charge (ASAC) Tim Weiss deciding he had an exceptional job for him. Or at least it was a weird one. Plus, there was some mention of a new partner or two.

Richard heard rumors of Kim Kupar, also known as the Tiger Lady. These same rumors about the woman her training agent Rex Moyer nicknamed Raptor pointed to an individual who attracted the strange and unusual, just like Richard. He knew her only in passing as Richard usually worked out of the sub-office in Tacoma. However, Richard knew the problems with rumors. He had been on the receiving end of false rumors for years.

The stocky—but not short—former Border Rat shrugged his shoulders. A while ago, Richard had learned to roll with the punches. He punctuated that thought with a slurp of coffee and made a face. This raw attempt at a caffeinated drink will wake him up, he thought.

Most of the other agents and employees had not yet arrived at work when supervisors ushered Richard into ASAC Weiss' office. Kim Kupar already sat in front of the manager's desk.

"You and Kim know each other through Rex Moyer and firearms training. However, you have always worked in separate groups, especially since Kupar here was one of the original Special Forensic Group members. Well, that ends today. Richard, you're being reassigned to the Forensics Group with Kim here as your partner."

"May I ask why, sir?" asked Richard. "Kim is off of training status, so wouldn't she be helping break in others to the group? She has all the forensic experience."

"No. It is because you both have a unique ability to become involved in weird shit, pardon my French, and still come out smelling like a rose," replied ASAC Weiss. "You both get things done, don't sit behind a desk writing reports to look busy."

"I heard through the grapevine this has something to do with an unfinished case of mine," said Kim.

Richard smiled at the slender but tall young lady. "Is

that concerning a rather large cat?" he asked.

"You can always tell the real investigators." Weiss said. "They always seem to nose around, keep their ears open and find things out."

The ASAC paused for a moment, then continued. "Sir Khan, the modified Bengal tiger from the Jade Eyes case, was seen up around Port Angeles. Richard, you made some good contacts up there during *That-Which-We-Cannot-Talk-About*."

Weiss looked at Kim to see if she reacted and saw she did not. He smiled. "I know, Agent Kupar, that you and ole Rex Moyer probably heard some about that weirdness. But this project is starting with the Bengal, who is now a sabretooth cat."

"Project?" Kim asked.

"Call this the Why Files Project, under the Special Forensics Group. Investigations with a big question mark go to you two." Weiss sighed. "We are getting way too much weirdness lately. I'll take a straight drug smuggling case any day of the week over what we have been getting."

Weiss tossed file copies across his desk to the two agents. "Richard, you are technically the senior agent, but I expect you to listen to Kim's scientific expertise. Especially when it comes to the zoological sciences."

"I take it we begin right now?" asked Kim.

"You got it. Hit the ground running, agents. We are getting a lot of uncomfortable queries. They are giving me grey hairs."

"Who do we check in with?" asked Richard.

"Me. You work for the Forensic Group, which is due a

new supervisor. Group Supervisor Salmon is on his way to D.C."

"Good spot for him," said Richard.

The ASAC smiled. "I have to agree. Now, time to leave. I have some other meetings. Just be safe out there, okay?"

Kim and Richard did what many a pair of law enforcement investigators do at the beginning of a new case in the Seattle area. They went to the local chain barista coffee joint.

As Richard slurped his coffee and Kim sipped her tea, they became more acquainted.

"You have a fiancé at the Woodland Park Zoo?" Richard asked.

"Yes. Hank Thomas. We are soon going to have a civil ceremony for insurance purposes. We may need his expertise with Big Cats since Sir Khan seems to be our first subject."

"We'll clear it through Tim Weiss. I don't think he'll fuss about what help we get as long as it results in closed cases and no lawsuits." Richard sipped his coffee. "Good idea about the insurance. I'd do the same."

"He had my back in the Jade Eyes investigation, that's for sure," replied Kim.

Richard looked at his new partner, a lithe and tall woman. "You still have bad dreams, Kim?"

"Yes. How'd you know?"

Richard shrugged. "Takes a person with nightmares to know one. When the sound of strife and conflict draws you, causes you to go into harm's way, you sometimes obtain baggage."

The two agents sat quietly for a moment. Then Kim spoke. "You have no wife, nor romantic partner, Richard. At least that is the rumor."

"Yep. I am a bit married to my job. So, I hope your soon-to-be husband will not get pissed if I call you at all hours to ask you something or drag you out of bed."

Kim smiled. "We had that talk before I accepted his ring. We broke up once before because of this job. That will not happen again. Someday, we may want kids. I know my mother is demanding them."

The two agents laughed.

"I think most mothers are that way, Kim. My mom is still bugging me also." Richard glanced at his watch. "Well, I guess it's time to put the old nose to the grindstone. The info in these reports will not be implanted in our memory through osmosis."

The special agents stood up from the table to leave. Kim suddenly stuck her hand out to shake, a small smile on her face.

"In a tradition Rex Moyer imparted to me, shake. Or as he would say, put her there, Pard."

Richard laughed and grasped her hand. "Lady, we are going to turn you into a Border Rat like the rest of us."

"Sounds okay to me, Richard."

From small seeds, great trees can grow. From humble beginnings, great partnerships can develop.

It begins.

FILE 2
LOVERS & LABCOATS

I s it alive?"

"After a fashion, Jeanie, yes." Barbara Bell glanced at her roommate as she answered. Jeanie's airhead blonde image belied a sharp mind, which was why Barbara could accept her as a roommate.

Both young women looked intently at the contents of the small terrarium. The glass protected it from casual hands, but if a viewer leaned close, a keen eye would see the faint, crimson veins pulsed with life.

"What do you mean, roomie?" asked Jeanie Vang.

"Well, it's a mixture of old recovered DNA mixed with some new DNA we harvested in the lab. We adhered it to a sample of what could only be classified as artificial flesh, again produced in the lab. Mix it all together, and viola. Life. After a fashion, like I said."

"So, the... flesh has some growing veins and vessels," added Jeanie.

"Again, you put to shame all those dumb blonde jokes, Jeanie." Jeanie lightly smacked Barbara's arm at the oft said comment and smiled. Despite their different backgrounds, they were friends. Barbara kept getting vibes that maybe Jeanie wanted something 'more' after Barbara had mentioned on more than one occasion she was polyamorous and bisexual. Jeanie had many a male admirer in the Puget Sound area but gave Barbara that 'look' which, in the young scientist's experience, meant she was interested in a physical way. Barbara had often wondered who or what she was primarily interested in sexually, which could explain her overwhelming interest in biology and zoology, both of the living and the dead.

"So, why did you bring your experiment home?"

"Well, Jeanie, this is just a small part. A bit of leftover, I guess you might say."

Jeanie frowned. She was working on a psychology degree as opposed to Barbara's work on a Master's in physical science. Jeanie understood laboratory protocols, especially when it came to growing life in a test tube or terrarium.

"It's not going to grow, crawl out during our sleep, and start eating us, like that old classic sci-fi movie we watched the other night?" A similar interest in such movies was a source of bonding between the two young women.

"No, Jeanie. It is not 'the Blob.' It is something... different."

"Okay, Barb. Let's stop with the mystery."

Jeanie's roommate sighed; how to explain what she planned to do while away from the university laboratories' confines? After all, she had been the one who had found a way to combine the DNA of the old dried-out sample of flesh discovered in China with the current living DNA of related creatures... or supposed associated animals.

"Well, I plan to create a womb or egg-like structure for this sample to grow in and see what happens. We created this in the lab. Actually, I did the heavy lifting. After proving what can be done, the lab proctor decided to freeze the samples and go on to something else." Barbara huffed. "He has no imagination or drive. He is just a university bureaucrat."

"So, you're going to try and grow that sample into... something?"

Barbara paused for a moment. She needed to explain what, to some, would be an arcane process. At least Jeanie was more intelligent than most people.

"Just as a male sperm and female ovum join to form a fertilized egg, a zygote, I hope to stimulate the cells on this flesh or skin tissue to behave much the same way. In other words, I hope that this sample has enough pairings of DNA to begin to grow into a viable being. It should be a simple life form, so a simplified version of a human womb should suffice for some embryo to form."

"How far do you plan to take this development?" Jeanie still had a frown on her face. Barbara knew she would have to be careful about how she 'sold' this project to her roommate not to start a fight. Barbara needed some privacy to finish this project to prove to Mister Stuffy how he was so slow and unimaginative.

"Just far enough to show it's viable. At least in the sense that if allowed to proceed, not be aborted, a creature would result."

Barbara took Jeanie's hands hers and looked into her roommate's eyes. She tried to present to her roommate the most caring expression she could, using every bit of mental manipulation. Barbara was very good at manipulating most people. However, she had never tried it on Jeanie, who she considered a true friend.

"Look, honey. I know I am asking a lot of you. No one likes their house turned into a workstation, not even in progressive Washington State. But this is small and will be kept in my bedroom. I promise."

Jeanie finally gently squeezed Barbara's hands and smiled with a twinkle in her eye.

"Well, I guess if that does turn into a 'Blob' and takes over your bed, you could rack in with me."

Barbara smiled back with her best smoldering come hither look she could muster. She sealed the moment with an unexpected kiss on the lips. "Thank you so much, roomie. I owe you." She paused and licked her lips. "Just say how I can... pay you back." Barbara thought sure Jeanie would try and use this moment to move towards a more physical relationship, with which Barbara would have no real problem.

Instead, Jeanie paused, winked as her mouth formed into a coquettish smile. "Let me give it some thought, roomie."

Barbara was busy the next couple of weeks setting up the artificial womb she had envisioned in the terrarium. Secreted in her bedroom, Barbara stole and scavenged material from the University while working on her master's dissertation at the same time. She noticed Jeanie was getting on edge with all of her concentration on The Project and no time even to have a conversation. The morning she saw Jeanie pouting, Barbara knew she had to do something to keep Jeanie from venting her frustrations to others. Secrecy was a key element at this critical stage.

Barbara hurried home from her university laboratory. She had stopped and bought an extra-large meat lovers pizza at the local student hang out. A weakness for meat on pizza (no anchovies) was another shared characteristic of the two roommates. Barbara called out as she entered the small rental house built in a bygone era but still comfortable.

"Hey, roomie. Pizza! Just like you..."

The front door shut from Barbara's butt push as she stood frozen and stared. Standing just a few yards away was Jeanie in a sheer black robe that left little to the imagination. Barbara tried to stutter out a comment but Jeanie spoke first.

"Well, roomie. Time to pay me back for putting up with your project." Jeanie winked as she smiled and the nightgown slid to the floor, black silk pooling at her feet.

The pizza was still on the floor near the front door, now cold, as the two nude young women lay in bed together, holding hands. Both roommates had smeared makeup, messy hair, and small hickeys all over.

Barbara remembered dropping the pizza and crashing with Jeanie as she kissed her. Then Jeanie took the dominant role, pushing the brunette against the wall and ripping her blouse open. The buttons popped and went flying as Jeanie went for Barb's bra and freed her beautifully-shaped breasts.

Barb was not quite as endowed as the blonde but Jeanie quickly focused her attention and the brunette was soon moaning with desire. Before she realized it, Jeanie had Barbara over the blonde's muscular shoulder and carried her to the roommate's bedroom. Jeanie had the scientist's shoes, jeans, and underwear—"These panties are now mine," Jeanie had purred—off in no time. Barbara began to respond more aggressively, playfully yanking the blonde's hair so Barbara could maneuver her over and allow the brunette on top.

Hands and fingers wound up between thighs, penetrating tightly trimmed curls to find very moist flesh. It became a contest to see who could make the other orgasm first. They both lost.

The two sweaty and exhausted lovers lay next to each other, exhausted but satisfied.

"I thought you might be bi, Jeanie, but... damn!"

"I thought you were interested, but no moves for some *three years*. I was beginning to get an inferiority complex."

Barbara turned towards her roommate and kissed her. Jeanie responded, then pulled back. "Hey. Should we talk about this, Barb?"

"Like how?"

"I don't do one-night stands, Barbara. In my early years as a cheerleader maybe, not now."

Barbara paused for a moment, framing her thoughts.

There was an odd stirring inside she had not felt before. "So, Jeanie, is this love, then?"

"Could be. All I know is I want to stay with you."

"Is that a proposal for some kind of bonding or marriage?" Barbara asked.

"Damn, you are so freaking analytical at times." Jeanie reached for her roommate and pulled her close until their bodies pressed tight up against each other. She held her mouth inches away from Barbara's mouth.

"Your move," Jeanie heavily breathed as she spoke.

Barbara licked Jeanie's lips with her tongue. "How about we say we are partners for now," Barbara suggested.

"Lab partners?" Jeanie asked with a giggle, then kissed Barbara. After a few moments, Barbara pushed Jeanie back a bit.

"So, you want to go the full shebang on my project?" the brunette asked.

"If I am going to share my bed with you in addition to sharing this house with an ever-expanding experiment, yes."

Barbara had a wicked twinkle in her eye. "My bedroom becomes ground zero for the great discovery."

Jeanie grinned. "And with that, we need to pause in lovemaking so you may show and explain to me *exactly* what you are doing."

The two ladies stood nude near a now oversized terrarium. Inside was an oval object that may have been what Barbara called a womb but what Jeanie quickly identified as an egg.

"Well, the sample from China may have been from egg layers, but no one is sure."

"Dinosaurs, Barbara? I read the Chinese are unearthing literal tons of fossils."

Barbara gently patted Jeanie's left butt cheek.

"Nice to have a partner as well read as you. The answer is, maybe. The fossilized sample was a bit—different—from the dinosaur remains around it, which may be why a minute bit of DNA somehow stayed. Those Jurassic movies have a bunch of B.S. in them. DNA and RNA degrade to dust over millions of years, impossible to type and reconstruct accurately."

"Well, then, did it come from a later era?" asked the intelligent blonde.

"That is the majority theory. Something was later feeding on dino bones and was also trapped and fossilized by another nasty event."

"So, what did you use to fill out the DNA strands so you could have a flesh sample?"

Barbara smiled at her lover. "You thinking about changing majors, Jeanie? You're talking like a biologist or paleontologist. I used a modern close relative to a T-Rex. Chicken DNA from a large Rhode Island Red rooster."

"I don't do things half-assed, Barb. If I'm going to be part of this, I need to know everything." Jeanie started to touch and squeeze the joints of the heavy-duty glass tank.

"You need some help in rebuilding this enclosure of yours. Especially if something hatches from the egg there, don't argue, Barbara. *That* is an egg. I think maybe some of your samples migrated while you were sleeping to help in modifying the shell."

Barbara snorted. "Too many movies, Jeanie. How can something that primitive migrate? I must have just mixed the right stuff for a shell, not a womb. And what do you know about construction techniques?"

Jeanie's mouth formed a sly smile. "I guess I never told you the whole story of the family business."

"Jeanie, I know your family owns a large car dealership. What has that to do with making glass or plastic containers?"

"Well, in addition to making some bucks so I can spend a lot on college, the family business meant I could hang around various repair and body shops. I was a little grease monkey, much to the consternation of my parents. They wanted me to be a 'lady' in the traditional sense. Greasy hands? Forget it."

"What happened then?" asked the biology and zoology major.

"I still hung around the grease monkeys, as I am just as stubborn as my father. I showed him that a little lava soap did not make my skin leathery, and I did not turn into what he called a 'dyke'."

Barbara frowned at the D-word. That was an insult she had heard before when she told people she was bisexual or polygamous and didn't dress 'feminine' enough.

"Your dad is a bigot?" Barbara asked.

"Just not enlightened. My dad hired gay mechanics if they could do the job. At the same time, he referred to people as Homo Hank and Queer Bob. We even had a Dyke Debby."

Barbara's face flushed with some anger. "Sorry, but your dad pisses me off. When I meet him…"

"Oh, so we are a formal couple. Great. I'll send out the engagement announcements."

"You are such a little smartass sometimes, Jeanie."

"Hey, lover," responded the blonde. "This ass is not little. It is nice, full, rounded and you love laying on it. Lighten up. Don't get triggered by little shit."

Barbara looked at Jeanie and once again realized she had been guilty of underestimating her. In the back of her mind, she had been the stereotype of a busty blonde airhead, despite the education Jeanie was getting. Plus, she was not pampered despite coming from a family with money.

"Okay, Jeanie. Point taken. Now, I have to see about maybe increasing my student loans to cover…"

"Stop right there, partner," interrupted Jeanie. "If I'm in for a penny, I'm in for a pound. I have bunches of money stashed away. My dad paid me for the work I did at the dealership and I won many a poker game. Guys love to buy blondes dinners and drinks, so my expenses have not been much. Other than the black negligee I bought to seduce you."

Barbara's mouth dropped open. "You little…"

"'Bitch' is maybe the word. Or perhaps 'cunt' is the word you are thinking. I've heard them all when you are supposed to be a dumb blonde looking for dick."

Barbara stood silently for a moment; this was going to be an interesting relationship. She felt the funny little butterfly feeling in her stomach and lower regions. If this was not love, it was close to it.

"Okay. Sorry I get irritated easily. I've had to work around who I am for quite a while. And my family is not well off. At the same time, I am not a charity case."

Jeanie turned towards her and took Barb's hands in hers. "Cut to the chase, Barbara. I'll be blunt like my dad. I do love you. I know you love me despite your confusion. Lovers help their lovers. So, in my spare time, I get the materials and expand your terrarium into more of a compound or cage for the babies I believe will come from that egg."

"For a non-biologist, you sure are certain of what is coming out of the so-called egg."

"Yes, I know. I can be cocksure, despite having a pussy instead of a cock. Now, let's take a break, eat some rewarmed pizza, then take a shower."

"Yes, ma'am! When does the dominatrix outfit come out, Jeanie?"

"Later," the blonde replied. "Only I think it may fit you better, Mistress."

And it did.

The weeks seemed to fly by as Jeanie built a state-of-the-art enclosure in record time. It took up most of Barbara's former bedroom. Both the women monitored the progress of the 'egg,' which was now the size of one from a giant ostrich. Barbara scammed a small surveillance camera with a motion detector alarm and helped her lover install it so they could watch the egg from the shared bed. Since Jeanie was graduating in the coming spring, just as Barbara would be presenting her master's dissertation, they were both already swamped. Thus, they had to fit everything into a tight schedule. Everything included lovemaking, which was a newfound joy for both.

One late night, as the two took a few minutes to caress each other's nude bodies, the motion detector on the camera dinged. Jeanie had increased the alarm noise to more of a loud ringing bell, so the two women leapt out of bed to shut it off. As they both looked into the heavy-duty glass enclosure, their mouths fell open.

"My God! Something is moving that egg from the inside!" exclaimed Barbara.

"Do we help whatever is inside break out?" asked Jeanie.

"I say yes. The eggshell may be too thick."

Jeannie dashed to the sleeping room and returned with a small craft hammer and a nail with that comment. The blonde used a surgeon's touch to poke two small holes in the eggshell, one causing a crack. No sooner did she do that, but something began to widen the gap.

"Quick, Jeanie, face masks. We can't chance passing human germs that may be fatal to a newborn."

"I'll just shut and seal this cage until we need to handle the specimen," the blonde replied. As Jeanie was doing that, a large section of the egg broke open. Then as the hole in the shell widened, the egg rolled over. The opening was against the sterilized soil on the bottom of the oversized terrarium as suddenly a snout poked through the hole. Then a second one slid through.

"My lord. Twins!" Barbara had no idea the egg could hold two viable creatures. For that to happen in the avian world would have probably resulted in dead or malformed young. Instead, the two living things broke the shell in half and stood to eye the area around them.

"Look at that, Jeanie. Both have bodies about six inches long, with about a four-inch tail. And they are bipedal, like a chicken."

"Or like T-rex," responded the blonde. "Their heads and jaws look like a miniature of the T-rex's. But those front limbs and claws look more raptor-like."

The lizards or dinosaurs or weird birds must have heard or felt the vibrations of the humans speaking as they looked thru the transparent glass at the blonde and brunette.

"Oh, my God," said Jeanie. "They have dog eyes. They are smart. I can tell."

As one, the two dark-colored creatures scrambled to the glass in front of the women and bumped into it; they then did what many a hungry hatchling does. They opened their mouth containing teeth-like structures, squeaked, and begged for food from their parents. Jeanie hugged Barbara.

"Look at our kids! Aren't they beautiful?"

"And hungry, Jeanie. What do we have to feed them? I didn't expect them to develop this fast."

Both women jogged to the kitchen and began scrounging up anything edible. After all, what did this new species eat? They looked like carnivores, but maybe they would want some plants. The two parents soon discovered they would eat almost anything.

"They liked that leftover fish," Jeanie said, her comment a bit muffled by the face mask.

"And the pizza crust and the meatballs and the Spam. They drink water like chickens, tilt their heads back." Barbara looked at her lover. "What do we name them?"

"Blackus Rexus after their true mother?" asked Jeanie.

"No, silly. What do we call each one?"

"You'll have to sex-type them first, right, Barb?"

"Oh great, Jeanie. Now I have to figure that out," complained the brunette.

It took the two roommates a while, but they could figure out one was male and the other female. Just like ducklings, the two little beasts imprinted on Barbara and Jeanie as their 'parents.' That made their handling, even with rubber gloves on, so much easier. Thus, they accepted examination, which led to gender identification in a general sense. Some quick research on reptile and avian diseases in captivity (what were they exactly?) and Jeanie made a short trip to a large chain pet store for supplies. They named them Freyr and Freya after the Norse fraternal twin gods.

The male Freyr had a small bump on his nose that looked like a developing horn. That made it easier to tell the two apart as they were identical in color and shape. They also had a thin covering of hair-like structures developing similar to some dinosaur fossils and the pair grew at a quick rate. Thus, Jeanie had the thick-glassed enclosure expanded to three-quarters of the former bedroom. Somebody must have squealed to the landlord/owner of the house as he came over asking if they were performing unauthorized modifications. Not to mention the methane gas farts the two produced, which wafted out whenever the roommates opened the enclosure. Jeanie stopped the investigation by a quick male fly unzip, some fellatio and a promise to return the house to its original state.

"Why didn't you ask for help?" questioned Barbara.

"Hey, the one knob-job for him is enough. If we gave him two, he would really be suspicious. Next, he'd have DEA in here looking for a Meth lab."

Graduation time came, and Jeanie graduated with honors. Barbara's Master's dissertation went just as well. The two scientists found some substances that acted as mild sedatives so that the two could go out and celebrate. Some friends tried to follow them home, but the now recognized 'couple' begged off, claiming they had their private celebration planned.

At some three in the morning, the two lovers stood by the large enclosure and looked at their sleeping 'children.'

"You did good, Barbara."

"No, we did good, lover. If not for you, they would have died in a cramped cage."

Barbara grabbed both of Jeanie's butt cheeks and pulled the blonde to her. "God, how I love you. It took me three years as a roommate to realize that."

"That and a lab experiment," Jeanie replied with a chuckle. "Barb, let's go to bed."

The next day, in the light of day and with two growing mouths to feed, Barbara and Jeanie realized they had to look into the future. They kept their parents away from the house during graduation by making some excuse of having to fumigate for bugs, but Jeanie would need to visit family and they both had to prepare for what would happen after summer. Barbara looked towards a university paid position as she worked on her Ph.D. while Jeanie would have to ask for some help from her parents to stay in school for a master's degree. No way did the two lovers plan to separate.

"I might be able to pass them off as mutant lizards or alligators."

"From where, Barbara? And how long will they live on their own?"

"Well, they can't get that much bigger, Jeanie. Some species grow to fit their habitat. The size of the enclosure may slow their development. That should give us some time to figure this out."

The next day proved the couple had no such time.

Barbara came home with a hangdog look on her face. She went into the shared bedroom and plopped down on the bed. Jeanie came from cooing to Freyr and Freya. The two creatures would chirp and sing back to one of their Moms like parakeets.

"Those bumps above their shoulders look a bit larger, lover... hey, what's wrong? Your face looks like you just lost your last friend."

"I was offered a kickass job at the University,"

mumbled Barbara.

"Hey, that's great! What's the problem?"

"First year is in China."

Time seemed to freeze. Jeanie sat down next to her lover.

"Fuck," the blonde said. Then she began to cry. Barbara joined her, and they hugged.

"You'd better wait for me, Jeanie," Barbara said between tears.

"Hell, yes. We can tie the knot in secret and you go overseas still single. The University doesn't need to know. I'll stay here and hold the fort."

"With the 'kids.' By yourself? And work? Go to school? What if they keep growing?"

"We are not putting them down!" snapped Jeanie. The two sat silent until Barbara broke the silence.

"Let me do some phone work tomorrow. I may have some off the grid people who may take them off the record."

"No goddammed experimental labs, Barb. Not like the government treated those chimpanzees a few years ago."

"Give me a chance. Okay? Just give me a chance."

Freyr and Freya began to chirp and sing like overgrown parakeets as they waited for food.

Barbara did not sleep well that night. She noticed Jeanie must also have had problems as she was out of the bed for most of the sleep cycle. Barbara finally woke up and crawled out of bed.

She found an empty house; Jeanie and the 'kids' were

gone. She screamed, then grabbed her cellphone. As the brunette started to hit speed dial, she saw the note taped on the enclosure.

"Sweetkins. Please don't be mad. I have a place where I can set them free. Mother Nature will decide if they can live. Love you with all my heart."

Barbara sat down and sobbed.

Some three hours later, Barbara heard Jeanie's SUV drive up. The enraged brunette met the blonde at the front door and tried to slap her.

"You bitch! I bred them! How dare you!"

Before they realized it, the two women were biting, scratching, pulling hair and kicking in a good old-fashioned catfight. Jeanie may outweigh Barbara some, but the brunette was just as strong. They rolled around on the floor, cursing and crying out of hurt and frustration. Jeanie dug her nails into Barbara's skin and Barbara clawed at the blonde's face to stop her and suddenly, the two grown women looked into each other's eyes and froze.

"What the fuck are we doing?" asked Jeanie. They shoved each other apart. Barbara began to sob. Jeanie reached over hugged her and she did not protest.

"Why? What did you do with them? I love you, Jeanie, but…"

"I took them to an abandoned farm I know near the Canadian border. That gives them a chance to die free, not in a cage."

"And if they don't?"

"Barb, they are creatures created in a laboratory. Do you think they can survive and breed? As it gets colder, they will fall asleep and not wake up, as dogs do on a farm. Trust me."

Barbara firally looked at her friend. "At least they won't be tortured by some asshole in the lab as they use them for test subjects."

"Barb, I love you. I was just trying to keep you from feeling the pain of having to make this decision. Please. Give me a chance."

The brunette nodded yes, then stared directly into Jeanie's eyes.

"Just don't do this again. If you do, I'm gone. After I kick your ass."

"Deal, lover. I'm sorry. Forgive me?"

"This time, yes. Just don't push your luck."

It took a few days for the women to clean up the enclosure and clean up their relationship. Barbara brought home a large bouquet just as Jeanie did. They laughed until they cried, then made soft love to each other as they began to repair the damage to their partnership. In August, Barbara was off to the University of Beijing as an official representative of the University. The two women were secretly wed and planned an actual ceremony when Barbara returned.

"Don't you go and screw some Geisha over there, lover," said Jeanie.

"Those are in Japan, not China."

"I know. I was just trying to see if you were

paying attention."

"And I'll be careful about any new virus from Wuhan."

They kissed long and deep at SEATAC Airport, screw any looks they might get from less than understanding people; then Barbara was on the plane.

It was the end of June and a beautiful sunny day in Seattle when Barbara landed at SEATAC International Airport. Via the wonders of the Internet (despite Chinese government censorship and surveillance), Barbara and Jeanie kept in almost constant contact. The brunette could not wait to see her love again and get her home for some 'alone time.'

Traveling with Barbara from China was Senior Professor Heng Tse from the University of Beijing. He had been instrumental in providing the original samples to the University used in the experiments. Tse also provided extra pull to keep them from being hassled about any virus quarantine. Professor Tse told Barbara he was impressed with her abilities when it came to genetics and would help her achieve her Ph.D. in record time. Everything was looking up as the Chinese National and Barbara entered separate TSA lines then Customs and Border Protection.

Barbara approached the uniformed inspector with a smile on her face. She handed the black female officer her customs declaration as well as her passport.

"What do you have to declare, ma'am?" the officer asked as she perused the passport.

"Some gifts and some reference material. I'm traveling with Professor Tse from the University of Beijing."

The Customs Officer frowned as she looked at Barbara's passport, then turned her face away as she mumbled something into the government radio.

"I hope my declaration is in order," Barbara said as she looked up to see three 'suits,' one male and two female approach from behind a cubicle partition.

"Ms. Bell? I'm Senior Agent Richard Johnson, Homeland Security Investigations," said the male. "You will need to come with us."

"What?" Barbara sputtered. "What is wrong? I'm... "

The large tall blonde female who made Jeanie look small growled at her. "Come easy or come hard. Your choice."

The third official was a woman who appeared to be part Indian. She presented a half-smile at Barbara.

"Come, Ms. Bell. You do not wish to create a scene, do you?"

Barbara sputtered, then allowed herself to be guided to a back office. Senior Agent Johnson carried her bags with the help of a uniformed officer. In a moment, a shaken Barbara sat with her back to the wall and faced what could only be a two-way mirror like she had seen in many a cop drama. The officer with the half-smile then spoke.

"I am Special Agent Kim Kupar, also of Homeland Security. My tall friend here is U.S. Fish and Wildlife Agent Brenna Freiberg. I will be interviewing your traveling companion Heng Tse as I speak fluent Mandarin Chinese. I suggest you be as honest as possible and your statements jives with his. Senior Agent Johnson will explain everything. Now please excuse me."

Barbara knew she was being 'played' by the three-agent tag team, but she was utterly flustered for all her training and experience.

"Look, sir, ma'am," she began, "I am not smuggling anything. I have not done a single illegal act while in China. I have no idea why I have three agents looking me over."

"As I believe a picture is worth a thousand words, here is a couple of photographs which should explain why you are here," said Agent Johnson. "That is before we give you a chance to explain."

The stocky but not short senior agent pushed two quality glossy photos towards Barbara. As her eyes focused on them, she gasped. The first was a cleaned-up photograph of a larger-than-life Freyr and Freya. It looked like the camera caught them while moving down a forest trail. The second photograph showed both of them coming right at the camera, mouths open and baring longer teeth than Barbara remembered.

"My God! They're alive!" Barbara blurted out before she knew better.

"No fooling," said Agent Freiberg. "And if you look close in the second photo, you'll see a smaller version of them behind them. The creatures had kids."

"I...I...we—" Barbara stammered as her brain overloaded. Their children were alive beyond all expectations, mated and reproduced. How?

"By the way, your wife, Jeanie—yes, we found the marriage license—said the adults' shoulder bumps appear to be morphing into wings."

Agent Johnson pushed a form towards her. "Here are your rights along with the basic crimes for which you are charged. Please read them. You have a Master's degree, so you should understand them, but feel free to ask questions."

"And by the way, the second photo is part of a video. They killed the photographer along with his wife and two children." The senior agent raised his eyebrows, adding, "Then your former pets partially ate them."

It was not the smartest thing to do, but Barbara began to spill her guts in between fits of crying. All she ever wanted to do was to create something no one else had or could create. Barbara had, and then people were killed because of her creation. She was Mary Shelly in reality, not fiction. As she went through another batch of Kleenex, Agent Freiberg spoke. "Your little experiment resulted in an invasive nonnative species to be inserted in a new habitat. Just like with pythons in the Florida Everglades, people and animals are put at extreme risk. Unlike the pythons, these creatures seem to be a new level of a predator, one of which we have no previous experience." The large woman brushed a loose wisp of blonde hair back. "To say I am incensed that someone with your education would do something so dammed stupid and irresponsible is an understatement." The agent glared at Barbara. "If I could, I would tar and feather you."

"Agent Freiberg takes her wildlife seriously," Agent Johnson injected. As he finished speaking, Agent Kupar reappeared with a handcuffed Professor Tse. He was tall despite his Chinese heritage, but he seemed to have shrunk during the questioning.

"The Professor asked to see Ms. Bell before we take him to confinement," Kim Kupar stated. "I had to explain he does not have diplomatic status just because he is from the University of Beijing."

"Please, Barbara," the professor began to blurt out. "Tell them I had no…"

Agent Kupar cut him off with flawless Mandarin. Barbara had learned enough Chinese that she heard Kupar tell Tse that whining would do nothing for him as the U.S. government had evidence that he had provided the tissue samples to the university—the tissue samples Barbara had modified. None of the material brought in had ever been declared or cleared by any governmental agency in the United States, especially after the COVID-19 problems… and the rumors that followed about secret Chinese labs.

Agent Kupar switched to English as she addressed the brunette scientist. "It seems you are brilliant in your work. I have a strong background in zoology and biology, and worked at the Woodland Park Zoo. I have only ever seen genetic manipulation like this once before."

"What was that?" Barbara managed.

"Another Chinese attempt to create an exotic animal," Kupar answered. "A sabretooth cat."

"That was real?" Barbara asked. She had heard rumors in the university's zoology system.

"It's still out there," Agent Freiberg growled out again. "Kim and I were supposed to go looking for it when this happened." She cursed under her breath. "Can you imagine some large cats in the Washington Forests, made for cold weather like during an Ice Age? They'll breed like rabbits."

"Well, this matter is more pressing," replied Senior Agent Johnson. "The sabretooth has only killed the people who tried to breed him, not some family of tourists."

Barbara started to blubber but caught herself. "Look—I confessed," the young brunette said. "I fucked up. I was playing with something I shouldn't have." She took a shuddering breath and asked, "But what can I do for Jeanie?"

"Funny you should ask that," Johnson said with a slight smile. "We were thinking of a field trip."

After the agents transported Professor Tse to the Immigration Detention Center pending decisions on whether to prosecute him or deport him, Barbara was allowed to clean up and put on some outdoor-type clothes from her luggage. Then the agents magically produced Jeanie. The two women were allowed to embrace and sob a bit before being separated.

"Your friend Jeanie here said she would lead us to the original drop-off point for your pets," said Agent Johnson. "And I believe these two raptor-like creatures bonded with you both from day one. Correct?"

The two women both mumbled yes.

"They come when called?" Freiberg asked.

"Yes," Jeanie said. "They'll talk to you like parakeets and parrots. If I whistled, they knew it was food time."

"They sat on our shoulders like hawks," added Barbara. "Putting them down would have been like putting puppies down."

"They were like... *family*," Jeanie said.

Agent Freiberg snorted. "Yeah. Wild homicidal puppies that kill and eat humans."

"I thought they would go to sleep and die during the winter months," Jeanie replied. "That's why I let them loose."

"You didn't realize that these creatures of yours had bird characteristics? That they are warm-blooded like some of the avians Professor Bell used for additional genetic material?"

"You did a workup on their DNA?" asked Barbara.

"I assisted in that exercise," said Agent Kupar. "However, you both are intelligent women and should have easily noticed they were not reptilian if for no other reason once they started growing feathered crests down their backs."

"Feathers?" Barbara looked at Jeanie with a confused expression on her face. "We saw some hair structures, no real feathers."

"A feather and some skin samples from under the fingernails of one of their victims. It helped us to determine who and what they are... and are not."

Jeanie's chin began to quiver. "I didn't want to hurt anyone or anything."

"You know," Agent Freiberg interjected, "for being so educated and intelligent, you bitches have no common sense." The large blonde lady turned and stomped off.

"I apologize for my fellow agent," said Kupar. "But she considers herself a keeper of all the wildlife under her purview. So, she takes this case involving an invasive species very personally."

"So now," added Senior Agent Johnson, "we come to the step where you two can help yourselves as well as deal with this mess you helped create. Time for a field trip."

The married couple was allowed to ride together in the back of a black SUV with dark tinted windows. The agents had escorted them to a secure area of the airport where several SUVs were parked. Standing around them were some dozen tactically clad individuals with blackened name tags and wearing balaclavas that covered their features.

Barbara whispered, "Those are not cops."

"Very observant," replied Agent Johnson. "They are members of a particular unit that helped me out of a similar situation up in Port Angeles. I suggest you follow their instructions if they speak to you."

Barbara shivered and Jeanie put her arm around her. Agent Freiberg set a long gun case on the hood of one of the SUVs and opened it.

"That's a capture gun, isn't it?" Barbara asked as Freiberg took the large rifle from the case. "You use that for large animals."

"Yep," the agent replied. "I have three special anesthetic loads used on crocs and gators as your 'friends' may be more warm-blooded but seem to be as aggressive as those descendants of dinosaurs you were trying to create."

"I count four shots," Barbara said as she leaned forward.

"The fourth will inject a binary acid into whatever it hits. You'll see why if we can find your 'kids,' ladies."

"Your job is to help us track and attract your creations," Johnson stated. "Then stay out of the way. If we can capture one alive, we will. If not...." The agent nodded towards the black-clad personnel.

Barbara and Jeanie rode in the rear seat of an SUV with Kupar driving and Johnson riding shotgun. The two women were not restrained; where would they go? Running off into the forest was not an option. Jeanie directed Kupar to the part of the northern woods where she had released Freyr and Freya.

"We'll meet a couple of Border Patrol agents up here," said Johnson. "Your creatures have been playing havoc with their border intrusion sensors. They were even smart enough to dig a couple up."

"They knocked down a drone also," added Kupar.

"How?" asked Jeanie.

"If we find them, you'll see."

Approximately an hour later, the group of four SUVs was soon well off the beaten tracks. On a dirt road that ran up a small gully into Canada, the group met a 'Mean Green' marked vehicle. Two Border Patrol agents were soon conversing with Agent Johnson. When Johnson pointed out the two detained women, one of the agents with the name tag Moreno marched over to the passenger side open window.

"I just wanted to tell you that your dammed monsters killed my K-9," Moreno spat with anger. "I hope you have a long time in prison to think about your stupidity." The Border agent then stormed back to his vehicle.

Johnson approached the two shaken women. "I guess I could have stopped him. However, I think you need to realize the seriousness of what you did in creating this species."

"How many times do we have to apologize?" Barbara replied with some heat.

"Don't apologize, lady. Just help us fix this fiasco."

One of the balaclava-wearing men had a sizeable mastiff-type dog on a thick leather leash.

"That's a large dog for a tracker," observed Barbara.

"That K-9 is more for takedown than tracking, "said Johnson. "Your creatures have not developed any fear of humans, so they have not tried to conceal themselves. At least not the adults and near yearlings."

"They bred that fast?" Jeanie asked.

"Some of the government experts believe your two beasties were gravid weeks after hatching or birth. That is another argument. Was that artificial womb you made an egg and do they lay eggs, or do they have live birth? Since no one has done a long-term study thanks to you hicing their existence, cell samples give clues but not a certainty."

Agent Kupar walked up with a pump twelve-gauge shotgun in each hand.

"As you requested, Richard. Loaded with five slugs."

The male agent took the offered weapon, jacked a round into the chamber, and engaged the safety. He saw the two civilian women look at the shotguns with a bit of tribulation.

"Agent Kupar took a Bengal tiger down in her younger years, and I grew up hunting, so no, we are not going to leave everything to our special black-clad friends."

"You shot a tiger?" asked Barbara.

"It tried to eat my uncle," the darker-skinned woman answered. "It went rogue, so we hunted and killed it on behest of the Indian government. Not much different than this situation."

"So, ladies," added Johnson, "you stay at the back with us; Agent Freiberg will be rear security with the capture rifle."

"So, shoot to kill takes precedence over trying to capture Freyr and Freya," stated Barbara.

"They kill people," answered the wildlife agent, "and should not exist here. So, treating them like mad dogs is the concept of the day."

The two women became very quiet.

The Border Patrol agents were trained trackers and knew the wooded area like the back of their hands. Their headquarters also had a surveillance drone up in addition to monitoring the border intrusions sensors upgraded recently. Barbara and Jeanie each had a small backpack with water and a couple of nutrition bars. As the women realized before, there was nowhere for them to flee, so no one worried about providing them items, making their escape easier. The two young ladies kept in shape, so they had no trouble keeping pace with the government personnel. Everyone walked in silence.

Just under two hours into the trek a radio crackled to life. The group halted as one of the Border Patrol agents talked with their communications center. Agent Richard walked up and powwowed with the Patrol agents and the leader of the special tactical unit. After a short conference, Richards walked back to the others.

"Several sensors hit right on the Canadian border. Another reason we need to take care of this problem ASAP. We need an international incident like—"

The oversized mastiff let out a deep rumbling growl, followed by a single bark. The dog pulled on the leash and began to drag his handler forward.

"Contact," said Richards. Then Hell arrived.

Something of substantial size glided down at speed from a tall Douglas Fir tree. At first, Barbara's mind said 'flying squirrel' then realized the figure was much too large. Before her mind could adjust, a small but intense fireball smashed into a brush next to the moving mastiff. The dog handler began to beat out flames on his leg, then dropped and rolled. The mastiff took off like a freight train at the flying object.

"Dragon!" someone yelled as weapons came up, and the armed personnel looked for targets. There was growling, barking and an odd screaming as the canine mastiff caught something that fought back violently. Then another fireball streaked down from a tall tree.

"Twelve O-clock high!" The warning was followed almost instantaneously by automatic weapons fire. Agent Freiberg shoved the two civilians to the ground as she brought the capture rifle up to the ready position. A black-clad warrior burst into flames as a new fireball found its mark. A comrade yanked a compact fire extinguisher from his pack and sprayed the downed man with foam before the fire spread. Then the shooting stopped, and an eerie silence engulfed the group of humans.

The bloodied mastiff brought his trophy back to his handler. Agent Freiberg grabbed Barbara by her arm and half carried her forward to where the carcass lay.

"Is that one of them?" the agent demanded.

Barbara looked closer at the dead winged animal. The colors were different, and the photos Johnson had shown her were of a much bigger individual.

"One of their offspring," Barbara heard herself saying before it sank in. Freya and Freyr had kids. They were very dangerous kids who could fly and spit fire. What had she done?

"So, they are flying dragons," said Kupar. "I thought it was all late-night radio conspiracy theories."

"We raised dragons," Jeanie slowly said in shock. "How?"

"The supposed flesh sample was of a dragon-like creature, not some dinosaur or recent reptile," replied Kupar. "And you helped the Chinese make another unnatural chimera. Like my sabretooth cat."

Jeanie let out a loud whistle, then a birdlike cry. Within moments there was an answering call from some thick brush. The tactical team used hand signals and were soon moving towards the source of the utterance.

"Let us contact Freyr," Jeanie protested. "I'd recognize his voice anywhere."

"You have nice pipes," said Richard Johnson. "But the only communication we plan on doing is to locate them so we can put them all down."

"No!" yelled Barbara. "They don't mean harm. They're predators just like us."

"Predators which fly or at least glide and spit fire. The scientists told us they manufacture tons of methane in their guts and individual bladders. They use some sort of internal chemical reaction to ignite it."

Barbara glared at him. "You had a specimen already, didn't you? You did not learn this from a skin sample."

"A small one caught itself in a large net; a fishing boat hung it out to dry and repair. It was chasing something and—down!"

Johnson knocked Barbara to the ground as a fireball missed her by inches. Agent Kupar's shotgun boomed three times and something seemed to explode in the top of a tree,

"Hit them when they have a full load of gas and they explode," said the female agent.

"Please! Let me try to contact our creatures." Jeanie pleaded. "They'll come to us; then you can capture them."

"They did imprint on us, Agent," added Barbara.

A short burst of automatic fire interrupted the conversation. Agent Johnson fixed the two women with a hard stare. "Go ahead and try. Did I tell you that these dragons breed like rabbits but hunt like wolves? So, the next step is an airstrike with napalm on this entire area."

Jeanie whistled loud and complex; she then followed with a human version of a chirping parakeet.

"Come to Momma," Barbara called out. "Freyr, Freya, come!"

A loud chirping and cawing from out of the forest quickly followed.

"See, I told you they'd respond," Jeanie lectured. "Just let us approach the pair we raised and—"

Other loud chirping and cawing came from a spot behind the group of humans. Then another batch of sounds from their left, then the right. A cacophony of sounds formed a circle around the Homo sapiens.

"Well, fuck me," Agent Freiberg said as she set the capture rifle down and drew her pistol.

FILE 3
SPASM

C ome, Baleen. There is someone you must meet."

Kim Kupar gave the man her most coquettish smile. Pedro De La O was a major Narcotrafficante who Kim spent weeks of intensive undercover work to gain his trust. To him, she was this mysterious Asian beauty who inflamed his passions just enough to get him thinking with his tiny head rather than his big head. Now, it looked like it would pay off. Pedro was about to introduce her to some high-level manager of another smuggling organization. Pedro had partnered with the other group due to the recent troubles. The Thing from Wuhan, the COVID-19 virus had shut down international travel so drastically that precursor chemicals, currency, hard narcotics themselves were hard to locate. Pedro said he had found a way to replace the necessary products he marketed. The Mexican-American had hinted to Kim—Baleen—he had a replacement drug to crystal meth, coke, and heroin. The Americas and federal law enforcement did not need another destructive and addictive substance.

Kim allowed Pedro to put his arm around her, and she

gave a playful squeal when the man squeezed her butt cheek. In the back of her mind, she knew the Homeland Security Investigations surveillance team was getting some great laughs at her having to put up with 'Mister Hands' as Pedro tried to paw her. Sex was out of the question, but anything short of that to get the information was not.

Pedro De La O steered Kim into a back room new to her. "What is this backroom, Papi?" Pedro liked her to call him by this pet name. Kim was hoping those listening through her earring microphones caught the fact she was in a secret back room. If things went to shit, Kim wanted help *now*. Pedro flicked on some subdued lighting in this new room. The special agent could make out a high-end stuffed leather sofa and matching love seat. Kim was about to try and wiggle out of any tête-à-tête when she noticed a man sitting in a matching leather recliner.

"Baleen, I would like you to meet Li Wei Zhao. He and his people have developed something unique. We call it Spasm."

The man rose and came towards Kim. The smile on his face disappeared in a flash, and the man named Zhao began to bellow at Pedro in Mandarin.

"Do you know who this bitch is?" Zhao realized he was speaking in a language Pedro did not understand even if Kim did. He switched to English.

"This is the whore who took down John Wang! She is a federal agent."

Pedro had an incredulous look on his face. "Baleen?"

The Chinese man yanked a pistol from behind his back

and Kim reacted. She performed a perfect Kalaripayattu front high kick. Her high heel shoe caught Zhao under the chin penetrating up into the jaw. The man tumbled backward as blood gushed from the hole. Pedro tried to grab his desired lover in a bearhug and suffered a backheel into his groin. Kim twisted from his grasp and followed with a front crescent kick to the man's face. Pedro fell to his knees. Kim snatched up the dropped pistol as a bodyguard burst in, a large revolver in his hand. The federal agent shot the attacker in the face.

Where the hell was her back up? Was the room shielded to prevent eavesdropping?

Kim grabbed the revolver from the floor, and with a pistol in each hand, dashed out the way Pedro brought her. She ran into a female coming around a corner and bowled her over.

"Officer down!" she yelled, hoping the surveillance team could now hear her and react. Angry bees buzzed by her ears, telling her that someone was shooting at her. Kim threw herself flat and looked for cover.

"Police! Federal agents! Drop your weapons!"

Never was she so glad to hear her partner Richard Johnson's voice. Hands were suddenly helping her up, and two other agents rushed her out of the office building of Aztec Imports.

Kim sat in the surveillance van, still shaking from fear and adrenaline rush. She sipped at the coffee. Then Richard was seated next to her.

"That was way too close, Kim."

"No, shit. What happened? Why the delay coming in?"

"That damn backroom must have been shielded from any radio waves. You went dead right after Pedro said he had someone he wanted to meet."

"The guy I shot…"

"He'll live. Professional Responsibility agents will grill you tomorrow, but ASAC Weiss told them to pound sand right now while taking you to the hospital.

"I'm okay, Richard—"

"No, you go to the hospital. Otherwise, everyone in the world will be giving you the third degree."

"What about Pedro? And what about this Spasm drug?"

"We have Zhao's cell phone. We are checking it now, trying to use it to pinpoint where the drug is stored. The wiretap said Pedro was to receive a shipment of some new stuff this evening. Somehow Zhao got in the building without anyone noticing."

"Hell, I have never seen him in my life. But he saw me somewhere. Maybe at John Wang's nightclub."

"We'll figure it out, Kim. Now to the hospital. ASAC's orders."

It took some great work by technical agents in the Homeland Security Investigations Office in Seattle to track where Zhao had been. They traced his movements to a very upscale house on Mercer Island. Records showed a financial holding company purchased the home the month previous. The board of directors listed Zhao as a member. All the windows were covered and there were now no comings and goings. Thanks to a court order, a flyover with motion sensing and infrared detection equipment displayed many hot spots that moved around. The agents obtained a federal search warrant.

Kim and Richard were in the lead on the warrant. The typical knock and announce, and then the law enforcement officers rammed the front door. A wave of stench hit the agents as they entered. They backed off and quickly donned Hazmat equipment. After the pandemic, everyone was nervous as hell. They went back in and found a horror show.

Cages of screaming and howling animals reacted to the humans' presence; they seemed to want to tear the intruders apart. Then the agents went to the basement.

"Oh, my God." Kim tried not to vomit and lost the battle. She managed to get her mask off and puked in a filthy bathroom sink. Humans were in the basement room. Or at least they were once human. Now they screamed and ranted in their filth. An entire federal Hazmat Cleanup Team came in as a still green Kim went over some medical notes discovered in a filing cabinet.

"Want to know what Spasm is, Richard?"

"Shoot."

"These assholes abuse animals and humans and get them all scared and agitated. They then remove the enriched adrenaline-mixed blood and, in some cases, the whole adrenal gland. They mix up a Devil's concoction, do some tweaks, and viola. Spasm."

"What are the results?" asked Richard.

"Super meth. Orgasmic delights mixed with

unsurpassed stamina and strength. Inject an athlete, where there is no test yet in the sports field, and they get a boost that makes steroids look like a cup of coffee."

"The farming of this crap from those humans and animals destroys the livestock."

"Yes, Richard. So, they have to find more animals, strays, homeless people, foster kids—" Kim puked on the backyard lawn.

"Easy, lady. Time to take a break."

Kim wiped her mouth. "Richard, all because the quarantines and control of the U.S. Border shut down their supplies of product and the means to make the product. So, they came up with a new drug to push."

"Unintended consequences, due to us being nasty monkeys, Kim."

"I'm gonna be sick again."

"I'll get you some 7-UP. It always settles my stomach."

"Make it a Seven and Seven. I might as well enjoy myself between puking."

FILE 4
PREDATORS & PERPETRATORS

John Peterson drove the 4x4 extended cab pickup truck up the unimproved Olympic National Forest road. The roadway was actually no more than a wide trail chopped through years ago to provide additional access into the forest northeast of Forks, Washington. He took it slowly; there is no reason to hurry on what was his next to last day as a United States Forest Service Law Enforcement Officer. Thirty years as a 'Forest Cop' was enough for anyone.

Sitting in the passenger seat was the reason John was making one last trip up the wilderness road. Karen Schmidt was a fresh-faced, tall, and recent graduate of the Federal Law Enforcement Training Center in Brunswick, Georgia. Some four months of training to be not just a 'federal cop' but precisely, a Forest Service Law Enforcement Officer, culminated in her assignment to the Olympic National Forest out of Port Angeles, Washington. Just three days on the job and someone decided John needed to one last trip into Their Forest.

The special agents and officers assigned to both the Forest Service and the National Park Service, their areas in the Washington Peninsula overlapping, considered the forest as

Theirs. They treated it with a reverence a city dweller would not understand.

"You see God and all his creations every day," John Peterson told all his friends and family, "so of course, we want to protect it from idiots who don't deserve to visit it. That is why we consider it ours."

"I bring you up here, Schmidt, to show you something we deal with all the time," John explained as he continued up the semi-overgrown pathway. "It should be gone in a week or so. But you'll see others like it if you stick around."

"I'm looking forward to a long career, sir," Karen said. "This was my dream job after the Army. Lots of trees, no sand."

John grunted a short laugh as he slowly drove around a final curve and stopped the Forest Service vehicle.

"What do you see up ahead? Look closely."

It took a few moments for the young officer to see what John was talking about.

"That is a heck of a camouflage job on that cabin. Somebody had some military training."

"Yes, ma'am. Post-Viet Nam, some troops used to come up here to just check out of society. All through the National Forest and National Park, there were small groups as well as individuals. Then, as they aged, there were fewer and fewer. Then, we had all the crap in the various Sandboxes. So along with the marijuana grow operations, more and more illegal shacks and other structures." John pointed at the cabin. "This one is slated to be torn down next week."

John edged the vehicle up until it was some twenty-five yards from the front of the cabin. He stopped the pickup and shut the engine off, frowning.

"Officer Schmidt, please get the twelve-gauge out of the back."

As the new officer jumped to comply—as one does when one is a newbie—she asked, "Trouble?"

"That door was shut and secured with a hasp and padlock. It's busted wide open. Grab some slug rounds as a nasty bear could have done that and still be there."

As Karen recovered the shotgun and the requested slug rounds, she asked, "Sir, don't you want to see if we can get Fish and Wildlife up here? I'd hate to kill a bear, especially with cubs over an abandoned cabin."

"You and I are more important than a bear. I know many of your trainees love Mother Nature, but I plan to retire in a few days. And you do not need to have a shortened career. Got it?"

"Yes, sir." Karen knew her trainer was the most senior non-supervisor officer around. She would need to yield to his expertise.

In a minute, the two enforcement officers were standing in front of the Forest Service vehicle as John Peterson loaded five slug rounds in the gun's tube magazine. He slowly racked a round into the chamber.

"Okay. Follow me up with your pistol ready," John said softly. "There may be two-legged beasties in there who needed a place to hide."

"Yes, sir."

John walked slow and steady up to the crude front

steps. He stopped and pointed to some huge and very odd indentations in the soft soil near the steps.

"Those are not bear tracks," whispered John. "They are too big and odd for a wolf."

"Cougar?" asked the new officer.

"Maybe… if they did not look so strange. Stay frosty, Karen."

"Yes, sir."

John was large even considering his Norwegian heritage, so he quickly mounted the steps in one stride and then was at the bashed-in front door. "Federal Law Enforcement," the senior officer bellowed. "Come out!"

Something dark and immense slammed onto John Peterson and sent him flying off the crude porch and within a few yards of the pickup. Karen stepped to one side as the large man was knocked flying and began to empty her pistol into the shape. She was a combat veteran, and her training took over as she fired and emptied one magazine, then went into an emergency reload drill. Karen let out her best military war cry as the veteran fought. Then she was dead.

John lay stunned. He started to sit up, training prompting him to reach for his holstered pistol. Blurred vision registered oversized teeth, and then… nothing.

There was only silence other than the sound of the crushing and cracking of bones.

Senior Special Agent Richard Johnson drove the Homeland Security Investigation SUV not because he had pulled rank but because he knew the route better than the others in the vehicle. In the front passenger seat was statuesque blond U.S. Fish and Wildlife Agent Brenna Freiberg. In the back seat was Richards assigned partner Special Agent Kim Kupar. Next to her rode a broad and muscular civilian near and dear to Kim's heart. Hank Thomas was Kim's significant other, but that was not the reason for his presence. Hank was a Big Cat expert from the Woodland Park Zoo in Seattle.

"If we need a large feline predator expert, Hank is it," she told the powers that be. Thus, Hank looked over some forensic reports with Kim while Richard drove and Brenna surveyed the forest and mountains of the Olympic Peninsula. Richard looked in the rearview mirror as he spoke.

"You two are awful quiet back there."

"It's taking a lot of time to sift through all the reports from the various alphabet agencies," Kim replied. "The FBI was involved because of the deaths of federal officers. The Forest Service, of course, is investigating the fatalities of their people. Then we have the National Park Service because the crime happened on the border of national forest and a national park, Brenna here is providing her expertise as this might involve wildlife."

Kim paused for a moment and met Richard's eyes in the mirror.

"And of course, there is Sir Khan and me."

"I'm glad you asked me to tag along," interjected Hank. "All these various forensic reports from all these different federal agencies are fascinating. Then you have the County Sheriff and the State Patrol. A definite cornucopia of opinions."

The Fish and Wildlife Agent snorted from the front seat. "Cornucopia! A fancy way of saying like assholes, everyone has an opinion. You should have heard all the arguments in my office when you asked me to be part of this investigation. Everyone wanted to tell me what happened."

"Hell, Brenna," said Richard. "We had to ask you along. You are a founding member of the Why File Project. Your involvement with Forest Dragon led to the formal creation of this little band of merry men and women."

"Well, I'm still waiting for H.Q. to give me an official blessing on my extensive involvement. Right now, it's case by case." As Brenna spoke, she unconsciously touched a small burn scar on the back of her neck, covered when she let her hair down. Actual fire-breathing dragons, even small ones, were no joke—especially ones that could glide like flying squirrels.

"So, rather than listen to the good-time radio," said Richard, "how about you two in the back tell me what you surmise so far."

"Ladies first," said Hank with a smile.

Kim grinned back.

"That's it, throw your fiancé to the wolves so they can laugh at me first."

"No laughing here, Kim," replied Richard. "We've all been around the block with strangeness."

"Okay, then let me try and summarize a crapload of reports, some involving actual crap."

Kim shuffled through some papers and then began.

"Three weeks ago, the two Forest Service enforcement officers were killed in the middle of the day on an unimproved access road, more of a trail in reality. They were some fifteen miles northeast of Forks, Washington, in the Olympic National Forest. They were an average of ten miles from the border with the Olympic National Park, which bends around the forest area. The sun was out; there was no rain or cloudy skies. The purpose of the drive was for familiarization of the area by a new employee. Although the employee newly arrived from the training center, she was a trained combat infantry soldier, with prior service in the Middle and Near East."

"So, she knew how to handle a firearm in combat," said Richard.

"Yes. The lady emptied a magazine from her pistol at the attacker before she was killed."

"Her training officer didn't get any rounds off?"

"No, Richard. Forensic investigations by all the various agencies point to the senior officer was attacked first. The trainee shot at the attacker and expended seventeen rounds of pistol ammunition."

"Hits?"

Kim paused for a moment before she continued. "Now starts the strange crap. The various examinations of the crime scene resulted in ten fired bullets recovered. I mean that the recovered hollow points were in a partially expanded or deformed state as if they hit something solid and failed to penetrate. Almost like what you see when you shoot rounds into a ballistic vest."

"Any others found, Kim?" asked the senior agent.

"It only gets weirder," Kim answered. "Three other bullets were recovered from nearby trees. Luckily the various forensic agents were good, and when they recovered those rounds, one had some hairs on it. Results from the FBI and Fish and Wildlife Lab say the hair is not human. It is some kind of animal, but…"

"Let me guess, Kim. The hair is not an exact match of any local or known animal."

Kim smiled. "You'll be a field zoologist yet."

"Well, Kim. What do the tests show?"

She looked at Hank. "I'll let the big cat person tell you."

Hank cleared his throat, then spoke. "We, Kim and I, expected it to be Sir Khan. Whatever killed the two agents ate a large portion of the senior officer, a John Peterson. He was near retirement when he met this—attacker."

"And Sir Khan had been fed humans."

"Yes, Richard. But we had samples of Sir Khan's hair and fur. Search warrants even turned up blood work on the mutated sabretooth. The DNA does not seem to match."

"But no grizzly DNA?" Asked Richard.

"No, sir. Based on the damage done to the cabin and the two victims, the attacker had to be as large as at least our favorite manufactured big cat. No local cougar could do the damage."

"The DNA we could recover does point to genetic tampering along the lines of what the Chinese did with Sir Khan, who started as a Bengal tiger. But the samples of the hair and some dried non-human blood point to an unknown species."

"Oh great," interjected Brenna, "more flying lizards. I wish asshole humans would quit effing with Mother Nature."

"So, my Fish and Wildlife friend," said Richard. "No chance of any native species?"

"I looked at the reports also," replied Brenna. "The damage done when the two people were killed don't point to anything smaller than a grizzly or brown bear. The bones weren't just gnawed on; they were pulverized. Thus, we have no real picture of the bite of this creature. But even grizzlies don't pulverize prey bones like this."

"So, we have a creature with a nasty bite that will eat humans. Any suggestions since our original target was ruled out?"

"A saltwater crocodile would have such a bite," said Kim. "But deep Washington forests are a far cry from the Everglades."

"They also don't gnaw or chew up bones," added Brenna. "They tear hunks of meat off and swallow."

"But there are indications of DNA modifications—wait a minute. You had some blood there."

"Yes," replied Kim. "There was a small blood trail of the perpetrator. One set of blurred tracks that were kind of canine-looking but way too big."

"You accounted for thirteen rounds of fired bullets," said Richard. "You found seventeen shell casings. So, where did four hollow points go?"

"In the creature to cause the blood trail. But the trail

disappeared rather quickly. And no, there was no rain or signs of other scavengers to lick up the blood."

Everyone was silent for a moment, and then Brenna spoke. "Just great. A beast that absorbs bullets and heals itself. A beast as big as a grizzly, it seems." The wildlife agent glared at the others. "Any signs of it flying and spitting flames, I'm out of here."

The four met Forrest Service Special Agent Tom Olafson at the local Narcotic and Smuggling Task Force office. The living embodiment of Eric the Red met Richard with a huge grin and equally sized handshake.

"Good to see you again, Richard. Sorry that it involves the death of some officers."

Richard introduced everyone to Tom as he remembered the last time they had worked together. That had resulted in Men in Black having them sign Non-Disclosure Forms on Threat of Disappearing. Tom gave Brenna a longer once-over.

"You have relatives around here, Agent Freiberg?"

"Ballard and Poulsbo," the tall Nordic-looking woman responded with a grin. She then proceeded to converse with Tom in Norwegian.

Richard could see this was turning into quite the reunion, so he interrupted. "I understand you have a local man you wanted us to meet."

"Why, yes. He's in his truck in the back parking lot with his pack."

"Pack, as in animal pack?" Kim asked.

Tom grinned. "You'll see."

The Forest Service agent escorted the group to the backlot. A large older extended cab 4X4 pickup with a homemade camper shell showed the travel results through many deep forest miles. From the cab exited a bearded man that made Tom Olafson look almost average-sized.

"It's Grizzly Adams," mumbled Hank. The man did resemble a larger-than-life version of the television character.

"Folks, meet Kurt Peters. We all call him Wolfman because of his unique lifestyle."

As names, greetings, and handshakes were shared, Kim asked. "I take it you have dealings with the local wolf population?"

"It is easier to show you than explain," answered the big man. He stepped over the camper shell and folded up an aluminum flap. Through metal, bars protruded one of the largest canine snouts Kim had ever seen.

"That is not an average Lupus," stated Hank.

"They are mixed breeds created by assholes who wanted to make a badass beast," growled Kurt. "So, they illegally poached some wolves and started screwing with their breeding to make wolfdogs."

"That never turns out right," said Brenna. "Why people can't let wildlife stay wild is beyond me."

The wildlife agent stepped closer to the truck. "Mind if I say hello?" Brenna asked.

"Go ahead. Odin here will let you know if he doesn't want your attention."

The statuesque blond stepped up, spoke some

soothing words, and was soon scratching the large muzzle.

"Huh, he likes you," said the Wolfman. "I rescue them and any injured wolves."

"I helped reintroduce gray wolves into Montana," stated Brenna. "Had to educate some ranchers and farmers on what they cannot do to wolves. It's a balancing act between wild predators and livestock."

Kurt turned at looked at Richard and Kim. "You two work with Rex Moyer and Kregg Sorenson."

"Yes, sir," responded Kim.

"They're friends of mine from the military. Kregg comes up and we teach tracking classes."

"You think you can help us track whatever or whoever killed those two agents?" asked Richard.

"Yes. People are trying to blame my pack here, say some of them are running wild," said Kurt. "*Bull*shit. The partial track Tom showed me isn't any wolf—or any other canine for that matter."

"We'll take any help we can get," said Richard. "Can we step inside the office and go over the photos and maps of the area? We reviewed the files on the way up. This case may take a while to discover the full story."

"As long as we catch what did this," said Tom, "I don't care how long it takes."

The group of investigators eventually broke for a late lunch. Just before they went to eat, Tom stopped and went back into his office.

"Wanted to show you something we found in an

abandoned grow site. Legalizing marijuana in Washington State shut down a lot of illegal operations."

Tom handed a beat-up flyer to Richard. On it was some lettering referring to a pit fighting ring as well as wild boar hunting. There were a bunch of handwritten notes Richard recognized as Russian.

"Translation of the Russian talks about when these activities were to start. Some damn Russians illegally imported some Russian boars a while back and let them loose. Now they are breeding with escaped feral hogs in the national forests and parks."

"Could a huge one have killed your two agents?"

Tom shrugged as he answered. "They can grow large enough and are nasty when cornered. But the boars would have left their hooved pig tracks around. So far, nothing."

Richard examined the flyer some more, then handed it back to Tom. "That flyer points to one other possibility," he said.

"What's that?"

"That they imported something else like the Chinese did with Sir Khan, the tiger. Something they did not want us to find. At least not yet."

The agents made plans to check-in their motel rooms, get some rest, and head out to the crime scene area at O dark thirty in the morning. Nobody commented when Kim and Hank bunked together. Hank had clearance for information sharing, so there was no danger in pillow talk.

As Hank and Kim lay together in bed, their

conversation turned to the eight-hundred-pound gorilla in the investigation, Sir Khan.

"Do you think he could have done it, killed those two officers?" asked Hank.

"He could have, but unless someone cornered Sir Khan, I think he would have sensed their approach and disappeared. The Chinese Triad taught him to kill and eat humans, but..."

"But what, Kim?"

Kim propped herself up on an elbow and looked at Hank. "He could have killed me, but he didn't. He is a one-of-a-kind created sabretooth cat with enhanced intelligence. After hiding all these months, why attack and eat someone now? And bullets would not have bounced off him."

"Not all of them, Kim."

"Yes, and the ones that did seem to penetrate, they leave us with hair and DNA samples which were not his. The smudged tracks don't come close to resembling a big cat."

Hank looked into his love's eyes. "And you have a special connection with him."

Kim sighed and lay her head on Hank's broad shoulder. "I know it sounds all weird and spooky, but when he was so close and looked into my eyes, I saw an intelligence I have never seen in a big cat, nor any dog. If he had lips and a throat like us, I think he could talk."

Hank put his strong arms around Kim's slender and muscular body. "Let's hope we can capture him alive and prove it's not him killing people."

"We can hope, Hank. That is true."

"Time to sleep, Tiger Lady. Just like Sir Khan."

The two kissed and Hank was soon asleep. However, sleep did not come so readily to Kim. The bright tiger's image the last time she had seen Sir Khan kept surfacing in her mind.

Finally, she whispered to herself. "Sir Khan. Where are you? What are you doing?"

Fitful sleep came to the special agent in the early morning hours.

The sun was just poking up above the horizon when the four law enforcement officers, the Zoologist, and the Wolfman met in the motel parking lot. Richard had cups of hot coffee for all of them. They discussed their plans for the day as they sipped at their cups.

"Well," began Richard, "I guess we go to the picked-over crime scene just to get an idea of where the killer, or killers, took off to hide."

"Think it could be more than one?" asked Tom.

"I am not discounting any possibility. I have this gut feeling that any creature did not get there under its own power. I think someone was hiding it there for future use."

"As for what?" asked Brenna.

"That old flier Tom showed me about hunts and dogfighting got me to thinking. Maybe someone was hiding a beast for a paid hunt?"

"What kind, Richard?" asked Kim.

"Maybe something modified like Sir Khan. The hair and DNA samples point to a non-native species."

Brenna snorted. "Like I said, flying dragons show up? I'm gone."

Kurt looked quizzically at her, but no one explained the comment.

"Well, times a' wasting," said Tom. "Follow me, and I'll lead the way to the area above Forks."

"No vampires twinkling in the sunlight, I hope," Hank said with a laugh.

The group made good time. An hour and a half later and the three vehicles pulled up to the taped-off crime scene. As the group slowly exited their trucks and SUVs, Kurt called out.

"Stay by your cars, please. I want to try something."

As the five others waited, Kurt Peters released Odin from the back of the camper shell. The massive half breed first sniffed, lifted his leg, then began to walk towards the taped-off illegal cabin. Odin froze. A deep rumbling growl started in the chest of the oversized canine. Kurt stepped forward and began to talk to the canine; Odin responded with a couple of loud growling barks but refused to move closer. Finally, Kurt took him back to the camper shell.

"Odin is known to chase bear," explained the Wolfman. "He's scenting something that confuses him and he doesn't like it."

"Well, let's just do a walk-through and see if something had returned," said Richard.

The six humans slowly surveyed the area, stepping over police crime scene tape. Then Hank called out.

"Tom, when was the last time any teams were out here?"

"About five days ago, why?"

"Come on over and look."

In a couple of minutes, they were all standing around looking at a large pile of human excrement.

"I don't think any of our people would come in here and take a dump," Tom said.

"Motorbike tracks. There," said Kurt as he pointed down at the ground.

"I can see why you teach tracking, my friend," said Richard.

"There are a couple of backcountry campgrounds nearby, at least within a few miles," Tom said.

"I can follow them with Odin, see where they lead," offered Kurt.

"You go, we go. We have the badges and guns," stated Richard.

"Do we need to leave anyone with the vehicles?" asked Kim.

"Tom, could you have a uniformed officer head this way to help keep an eye on this until we get back?"

"Let me try."

Richard turned to Brenna, Kim, and Hank. "Dig out the twelve gauges and slug rounds. We'll assume there will be a creature the size of a large bear. The slug rounds should handle a similar beast. And bring water bottles."

Within ten minutes, the group began the search. Kurt walked Odin around the crime scene so he could use the wolf hybrid during the tracking. Odin had no problems following the motorbike tracks through the woods with Kurt. With the professional tracker in the lead, the group made good time. The trail soon led away from the campgrounds, which led the agents to believe the motorbike did not come from a group of campers.

The sun was at the midway point in the sky when they heard a motorbike engine. The six quickly found concealment as the vehicle drew near. A single motorbike with a single rider was soon passing the group. Tom reached out and snatched the man from his ride as if it were an everyday occurrence. A large hand over the mouth shut down any cries for help. They backed off the trail and found a small clearing. There, they began questioning the young man and found his I.D.

"All right, Mr. Jack Moore," began Tom. "You are using a motor vehicle in a prohibited part of the National Forest. You went into a taped-off crime scene area and defecated at an unauthorized area. You are not a bear that can take crap anywhere it wants. So, what are you doing out here?"

"I want a lawyer."

"Buddy, a lawyer will not help you. We caught you in the act and can seize your crap as evidence."

"I want a lawyer," the greasy-haired Moore stated once again.

While Odin sat and growled at Moore, the group talked out of earshot.

"We cannot let him contact whoever he was

meeting," said Richard. "If there is an animal involved, they'll disappear with it."

"Then some of us need to take this guy out of the area and the rest follow the trail," said Brenna.

"I can track with Odin. Who wants to come with me?" asked Kurt.

"Kim and I will," replied Richard. "Hank, you go with Tom and take Moore, keep him on ice. Brenna, you want to come with us?"

"Hell, yes. If these people are screwing with wildlife, I want to kick them in the ass."

"Alright. Tom, rouse some extra help also in case it turns out to be a large group with a bunch of beasts."

"Will do. I'll get an air unit up."

"Hold up on doing flyovers just yet. That will tip Moore's buddies off and they may scatter, plus release any animals they have. Our radios are working, so I'll scream if we need help."

"Gotcha."

Ten minutes later and the four hunters continued moving. They took it slow, easy and quiet. They didn't know what they looked for, only that the people they were dealing with had helped kill two law enforcement officers. An hour later, as the sun made its way across the afternoon sky, the four heard loud voices in an argument. Richard listened and realized it was in Russian. He signaled to the others, and they crept slowly forward.

They soon saw through the trees and brush two men arguing. Then two others walked up and began dressing them down in English.

"Will you two shut up in Russian and speak English?" a middle-aged man stated.

"I want to know what is going on and I don't speak Russian."

"Josef is saying," a young dark-haired man said, "that we still cannot find the one escaped beast. He wishes to blame me—"

"It is your fault, Peter. You left the cage open and did not feed it the sedative," Josef replied.

"It was your turn to feed the beast, Josef!"

"You left the cage open, you fool."

"*Shut up!*" the middle-aged man bellowed at the two Russians.

"Goddamnit, I never should have gotten involved with smuggling things in here. We are about to get caught with just one hunt under our belt."

"You do it, Michael Moore," interjected Josef, "because, like us, you desire money. And our organization has provided you money, more money than you would have made with your local dog fighting pit."

"Oh yeah? But at least I can get and breed dogs, keep them in normal cages. Unlike these—things—you have brought in on my fishing boat."

Peter spoke up. "Where is your brother Jack?"

"I sent him back to check on the cabin where the bitch was last seen. Pregnant dogs often go back to a favorite place when it's time to whelp. I hope there is enough dog left in your 'things' that she acts the same."

Brenna looked at the others in horror. "Another manufactured species let loose?" she whispered harshly. "We have to stop this now!"

Richard looked at the others. He knew that under the right circumstances, they would wait for backup. But if he did not act now to contain this potential disaster now, the U.S. could be facing a new and unnatural predator.

Kurt pulled out a .44 Magnum from under his camouflaged jacket. "Odin and I can help," he whispered.

"Well, fuck!" Richard said. He used hand signals to point out positions for his band as the miscreants kept arguing.

"If you Russkis hadn't let the bitch loose, we would be just fine," continued Michael Moore. "We keep the beasts hidden in the national forest and park until we have a hunt or a fight on the timberland we bought—"

"*Russian money* bought," interrupted Josef. "You Americans always forget who does what, as if you can do everything yourselves."

"Look-it, Josef. Just get some help so we can round up the Bitch and—"

"*Federal Agents! Police! Freeze, assholes!*" Richard used his best bellow as he and the other three broke concealments. Moore and the other unnamed American froze. The Russians did not. Both Josef and Peter threw themselves down to the ground. Bullets began to fly as they produced concealed pistols and started shooting.

The man with Moore began running and Moore yelled out, "Pauly, stop."

"Fuck!" Richard swore as he fired at the Russians with his twelve gauge. Now he wished he had buckshot instead of slug loads. Kurt's .44 Magnum pistol boomed along with the other agent's weapons. Odin exploded with a series of snarling barks.

Brenna went full berserker shieldmaiden on the scene. She burst from cover, screaming at the Russians as she emptied her pistol at them.

"No more flying fucking dragons!"

Kim cursed and joined her. Sometimes a full charge and assault work.

Brenna's shooting was accurate as she hit both Russians. The shooting stopped as Moore screamed, "Don't shoot! We surrender."

Richard and Kurt broke cover and advanced on Moore.

"The Russians are dead," Kim called out.

"Good," Brenna spat out. She strode over to Moore as Richard handcuffed him. "Where are the animals? Huh? Or do I have to get nasty?"

"I'll use Odin here and find them," said Kurt. "And that Pauly character."

"How did he dodge all the flying lead?" asked Richard.

Odin snarled and growled as he suddenly turned and faced a clump of dense underbrush. Kurt frowned. "Something... *nasty* is here."

A new voice yelled from some more distant trees. "Say hello to our not-so-little friends."

"Goddamned Pauly," Moore suddenly sobbed. "He let

the beasts loose." The man slipped to his knees and began praying.

"Beasts? More than one?" said Kim.

Oversized snouts filled full of crooked teeth poked through the brush. They had somewhat canine characteristics but with a macabre difference.

"Are those mutated hyenas?" asked Kim.

"Yes!" sobbed Moore. "Oh, Lord. We are dead. Please forgive me…"

"Shut up," snarled Brenna. She unslung her shotgun. "Well, fuck me. Again."

At least a half dozen beasts charged the humans. Odin met the first one, stopping it in its tracks for a moment, then was bowled over. Kurt used his Magnum on the creature.

The agents fired, hitting home with their shotgun slugs. However, these were not normal hyenas. These were monsters on steroids.

Kim was flattened to the ground by a shot hyena beast and once again saw a tooth-filled face of death inches away.

Suddenly, a furry dark-striped wraith slammed into the hyena and Kim heard a snarl and growl she thought she would never hear again. Then Hell visited the Hyenas.

Somehow the humans managed to untangle themselves from the attackers as the man-made creature named Sir Khan demonstrated who was the actual Apex Predator of the forest. Huge paws with sharp claws smashed and slashed the mutated hyenas. Kim watched as the sabretooth cat sank its oversized teeth into the throat of the largest one, twisted his tiger neck, and nearly removed the hyena head from the body.

Then it was over. Sir Khan stood alone among a group of bloody animal bodies. The great cat turned and looked directly at Kim.

"Sir Khan," she whispered. Richard started to raise his shotgun and Kim shoved the barrel down.

"No! Sir Khan saved me. He saved us."

Odin, the wolfdog, stood and stared. The sabretooth cat ignored the canine presence as he turned and let out a typical tiger cough. Then, in one silent leap, he was gone.

"A fucking ghost beast," Kurt said. "A spirit animal." He looked at Kim. "He is your totem. Always remember that."

Moore crouched, sobbing in fear. Richard keyed his radio.

"Sector   Control,   Sector   Control,   Emergency transmission..."

Customs and Border Protection Blackhawks and other helicopters were soon buzzing the area. Then a couple of unmarked all-black Blackhawk copters arrived, and black-uniformed personnel with balaclavas covering their heads fast roped into the site. Richard received a cellphone call from the Special Agent in Charge, telling him and the others to stand down. Richard had been through this drill before. Someone had an interest in the hyena-creatures beyond the evidence of a crime.

The team was allowed to transport Moore from the area as the dead beasts were bagged, tagged, and taken out by the black-uniformed personnel. Tom Olafson obtained some ATVs and shuttled them in with Hank. Thus, the group of agents was able to exit the forest as darkness fell.

As they reached the cabin where it all started, Kim pulled Hank, Brenna, and Richard aside.

"The pregnant female was not among the dead."

"How can you tell?" asked Richard.

"I was able to check each of the bodies. They were all males. I know my hyena morphology."

"So, we have a mutated pregnant creature out there which killed two federal officers. Great."

"But the people who caused that situation are either dead or in custody. Pauly was stopped by some National Park agents responding to our emergency call. He made the mistake of putting up a fight and received a bullet in the leg. Letting those beasts loose on us means he will be charged with attempted murder in both federal and state courts."

"So, he and Moore will have a good reason to cooperate."

"Yes, Richard. So, we can shut the Russian organization down."

"Yes. But we still have a vicious creature running loose. Not to mention questions about Sir Khan."

"I know. I still hope we can capture Sir Khan alive."

Richard sighed. "I am going to have a hell of a time trying to explain to the bosses how a formerly man-eating sabretooth cat came to our rescue."

"I'll help with my zoological expertise," said Kim.

"Would it be that easy. But we can try, Pard, we can try."

As the group was packing up and putting Moore in a caged vehicle for transportation to lock up with his brother, Hank pulled Kim aside.

"You okay, Tiger Lady?"

"Thanks to Sir Khan, yes."

"He must have been following you."

"But why, Hank? He used to eat humans."

"I think down deep, you know why."

She hugged her love. "Kurt said he is my spirit animal, my totem."

"I've heard stranger things, Kim. For whatever reason, I thank God he was there to save you."

"Yes, Hank. And I am, as is Brenna, thankful for one other thing."

"What is that?"

Kim looked into her love's eyes with a smile on her face. "No more damned fire-breathing flying dragons."

A week later and Richard was still writing reports as the official case agent on what was now called Operation Fighting Pit. Homeland Security had latched onto the plans' story to smuggle animals in for fighting contests as the primary focus. The fact that giant mutated Hyenas were involved, with one still running loose, was downplayed and buried as soon as possible. Officially including Brenna and

Hank, Richard and the team received praise for finding and breaking up a Russian pit fighting and smuggling organization. He received grief that it almost went South when he decided to attempt an arrest before backup arrived. Richard and company were praised for taking down all those nasty beasts and humans, with little mention of Sir Khan's timely arrival. Then, Sir Khan became a source of criticism as to, "Why was he not shot or captured?"

Richard grunted. Praised one moment, damned the next. So was the life of a federal agent. It could be worse, he thought. One of the team members could have been seriously injured. Then he would be on an extended TDY to Bumfuck, Alaska.

The desk phone rang. Richard answered, wondering who would be calling him at the office after hours.

"Senior Agent Johnson. Hey, hi, Tom. Nah, just doing the paperwork. As they say, the crap ain't finished without the paperwork—what? You found what? Where? Hot damn. Let me see if I can get up there to Port Angeles. Great news... I think."

The pregnant she-hyena was circling a campground in the Olympic National Park when her life ended. The creature had finally managed to scrape and tear off the Kevlar body armor the humans had fitted on her as an experiment. Sir Khan pounced and sank his saber teeth into her neck, then snapped it like a twig. She may have be the size of a small grizzly, but Sir Khan was larger than life... and *powerful*. The sabretooth cat had a family to protect.

The big cat quickly dragged the body over to a tent whose occupants were in the throes of two-legged monkey sex. Sir Khan had seen, smelled, and heard it many times before. It was one thing he had in common with humans. He liked sex also. Of course, when one of them exited the tent and fell over the body, things might not be so pleasant.

Sir Khan made his way up the slopes of the Olympic Mountains to a cave he had located. In that cave were his mate and four cubs. The female cougar was larger than average and had been able to carry the sabretooth cat's oversized offspring to term. The extended canines were already beginning to show. By bringing meat to her as part of Sir Khan's lion DNA, which promoted social pack behavior, the typical solitary female cougar eventually accepted that this male was around to help, not harm, her offspring. They became one big happy family.

Sir Khan stopped and thought about this odd female human he sensed and felt drawn to protect. Would he meet her again? Sir Khan did not know. What he did know was that the bi-pedal monkeys would be back looking for him. They always were. He would be ready, for he was an apex predator.

Sir Khan paused and let out a roar new to Washington's Olympic Mountains, the roar of a hunting tiger.

FILE 6
LEGION

Rhoda Roberson prided herself on being a traditional, no-nonsense 'Just the Facts, Ma'am' reporter. Screw the advocacy journalism with all those talking heads on the boob tube; she followed stories where they took her. It offended her when news stories were tweaked or ignored because of others' personal opinions or politics.

"You're awfully young to be a dinosaur," her news editor, Perry Jones, told her when she once again pushed for the publication of some story bound to smash political toes. The once-daily newspaper and now an online and print weekly news periodical named *Northwest News and Enquirer* was her home for the past nine years. Rhoda worked as an intern while getting a degree in journalism from the University of Washington. Thus, unlike many of her classmates. Rhoda had a job waiting for her upon graduation.

Rhoda was much taller and broader than the average professional woman in Seattle, did not have the desired Victoria Secrets model look, nor an on-air talking head position. Thus, few people tried to bully her or look up her dress when she came calling and snooping for a story. Rhoda was also a fan of Gonzo Journalism, where you lived and immersed yourself in the story. She had scammed assignments training with SWAT teams, MMA Fighters, parachute jumped with a U.S. military Airborne unit, and once even spent some time with a notorious Hispanic street gang.

She was a dog with a bone when she heard rumors of a Why Files Project in federal law enforcement. At first, Rhoda thought someone was making a joke based on a cult classic television series. Then, while hanging out at a dive bar, which was a 'demilitarized zone' between cops and crooks, she heard the term 'spooky cases,' and then the name Kupar. A quick check of the last name turned up a Homeland Security Investigations Special Agent Kim Kupar and a shoot-out at a downtown nightclub. Additional information mentioned an escaped smuggled Bengal tiger. Her name and a Special Agent Richard Johnson popped up in a story about a Russian animal smuggling operation near Port Angeles. A back story alleged illegal genetic experiments on some of the smuggled animals to create monsters. Now, maybe there *was* a reason for a Why Project.

Rhoda knew better than to go to the agency Information Officer, as she would get a smile and a blow-off. She reasoned the agents worked out of the primary Special Agent in Charge Office in downtown Seattle. With that concept, she took a recently retired federal agent out drinking. The agent tended to gossip, so it was easy to get her talking.

"It's no secret," retired agent Megan White said.

"Everyone wanted to get into Kim Kupar's pants. She's gorgeous."

"What about Richard Johnson?" Rhoda asked after ordering another round.

"He was more of a loner. Not bad looking, but didn't seem all that interested in tapping any of the local talents, if you get what I mean. I never heard of him being married or anything."

"Did he have the hots for Kim?"

"Not that he let on. He was all work. Kim has a fiancé; I think I saw a wedding announcement in the local newspaper."

"But Richards and Kim worked together on cases?"

"Eventually. Kim almost got herself fired over an affair with a Chinese Triad member, John Wang. You know the story about the big shoot out at the Asian nightclub, human trafficking and all." Megan finished her drink, then kept talking. Rhoda signaled the barkeep for another as the retired agent continued.

"I seem to remember seeing your byline as a co-writer on a follow-up article on the whole human trafficking thing," said Megan.

"Yes, I had some contacts with various human rights groups working the sex trafficking angle. But I heard there was a special Bengal tiger involved."

Megan shivered in her seat. "God, don't remind me. One of the last reports I did before retiring was a follow-up interview with some sex trafficking victims of ole Mister Wang." A somewhat drunk Megan laughed. "I heard Wang had a big wang, if you get what I mean. I guess that's why Kim got hooked—"

"We were talking about the tiger and the trafficking victims."

"God, you would make me talk about that. A couple of the girls who were smuggled in met this big cat—they said it was to scare them into cooperating, not running away from the massage parlor. They also stated this Sir Khan, the name they used, that the Chinese Triads fed the big cat people if someone pissed off ole Wang with the large wang." Megan gulped some more of her drink. "That image still gives me the creeps."

"A large wang gives you the creeps?"

"No, silly! The investigative crime scene photographs."

"There were pictures of that activity?" asked Rhoda.

"The crime scene photos were all blood and guts around a humongous cage. The blood was not all caused by Rex Moyer's bullets, especially since there were a couple of decapitated bodies."

"Why wasn't this reported before?" pressed Rhoda.

"Hell, the goddammed tiger escaped. Rumors are it's running around the Kitsap Peninsula. No federal agency wants to admit they let a maneater loose." Megan waved at the barkeep for another. "But you did not get that from me. I want to keep my retirement, thank you very much."

The retired agent stuffed some bar popcorn in her mouth. "After that, Richard and Kim were partnered up. They were coming and going, talked a lot behind closed doors with the bosses. I heard they had a special identifier on their investigation case files. Some of their ROIs, reports, were restricted access."

"So, they were real—Why Files?"

Megan shrugged. "Rumors." Taking another sip, she added, "I'll have to admit, Kim made me a bit hot when I looked at her... if you know what I mean. If I knew she swung both ways like me, I'd suggest—"

"But they worked on strange cases?" Rhoda interrupted.

"I guess. How about another drink? You can tell me what gets you all hot and bothered."

Rhoda called it a night as soon as she could; Megan seemed to be looking for any port in the storm, gender unimportant. In between 'make-work' assignments by Jones, Rhoda started bird-dogging the HSI offices as best she could without being jacked up by agents for interfering with enforcement work. After all, Freedom of the Press and all that.

Rhoda finally caught the agents eating lunch at a well-known Chinese restaurant in the International District, still called Chinatown by many in Seattle. Not being a shrinking violet, Rhoda walked up and introduced herself. Then she asked, "So, what about the Why Files? Which one of you is Scully?"

Kim Kupar gave her a professional smile and replied. "Please contact our Information Officer, Lori Danner. She'll be happy to explain any ongoing projects, as long as the information doesn't conflict with any open investigations."

Richard Johnson gave her the, "Hey, we're eating here!" look.

Rhoda gave them her business card and left. The next day Perry Jones walked up to her desk as she was finishing some fluff piece filler story.

"You got something going with Homeland Security?" the senior editor asked.

"Maybe. The agency has some hush-hush sub-unit over there. The agents allegedly assigned keep popping up on some weird cases."

"Like what?"

"Exotic animal experimentation, shoot-outs involving human trafficking downtown, busting people with illegal Virus Vaccine Labs, reports of prisoners disappearing from lock-up through blue lights."

Jones looked at her and grunted.

"Okay. Be careful. I don't want to bail you out of federal jail."

He started to walk away, then turned back. "And we are not the *National Enquirer*. No Bat Boy stories."

"That was *Weekly World News*. And yes, boss, I'll be careful."

Rhoda spent the next day perusing the Internet on *The Jade Palace Shoot-Out* investigation. Just as Megan had stated, HSI buried the Bengal tiger story under a lot of human trafficking stuff. A couple of paragraphs on other exotic animal smuggling appeared, but the government pushed the rescue of sex trafficking victims from China.

Rhoda then went to the federal courthouse and

examined the public court documents of the prosecutions which followed. Again, mentions of the Bengal tiger disappeared. The illegal Corona Vaccine case made a splash, but everyone pled out. Rhoda called a contact she had at the Woodland Park Zoo to talk about a big cat running loose. The connection told her to contact Hank Thomas, who was attached to Kim Kupar. Rhoda was not ready to brace Agent Kupar's significant other. She did not want the wrath of a tough female agent on her butt.

The next day, Rhoda tried to play shadow to the two agents. She followed them as Kupar drove them around in a government Ford Mustang. The two went to the local DEA office, the King County Jail and then back to their office. Rhoda couldn't follow them into those locations even with her press credentials, so all she could do was wish she was a fly on the wall. Besides, she didn't want to tip them off as to just how much she was bird-dogging them. She had some contacts at the county jail, so she would try and ply them with a drink or two. It worked with Megan.

Rhoda went to her office, organized her notes, and planned her next moves. Too bad she couldn't arrange an interview with Sir Khan. However, she might be able to scam a trip out of Perry to the Olympic National Park, as rumors were of big cat sightings of something not a cougar.

Rhoda drove home in her used Prius. As she exited her car in the driveway of her small duplex in West Seattle, a man with a suit wearing an N95 face mask walked up to her carrying a clipboard. Even with the vaccination protocols, there were still people who wore masks everywhere. The man had a nametag proclaiming 'Scientific Research Corporation.'

"Hey, mister. I gave at the office," said Rhoda. Then he tased her unconscious.

Rhoda was unsure how long she was out. The reporter had the funny taste one gets after someone uses anesthetic gas on them. The taser was just to stun her, then some gas to put her out. Rhoda looked around the area she was in and decided it was a basement room. Not what she expected from a Men in Black Operation.

"Hey, buddy. How about something to drink?" she called out as she tested the padded handcuffs restraints. These people bought their supplies at some adult sex store for sure. This activity was not something Rhoda thought was SOP for a government operation. The same man with the clipboard walked in and put a glass containing a liquid darker than water in it. Rhoda drank from it as her mouth and throat were so damned dry. After Mr. Suit pulled the glass back from her lips, Rhoda said. "Rum and Coke? Mixing that with knockout gas? Is that safe?"

"Reports are that it loosens the tongue," the man replied.

"What reports? And what am I supposed to call you? Agent?"

The man laughed long, hard, with a bit of hysteria at the end. "You think I am with the government? I am not part of *that* conspiracy."

Rhoda had a sinking feeling in her stomach. My God, she was kidnapped by the Aluminum Foil Hat Squad. At least government agencies had some rules, even if they often violated them. Nutzoids had few... if any.

"Sir, do you have a name?"

"You can call me Legion, as I am many."

"And you grabbed me because..."

"You're going to tell me the secrets you obtained from Mulder and Scully, the two agents working the special investigations in Homeland Security. I saw you talking with them and others."

"Just how long have you been following me?"

"Enough to know that you know what I need to know so that I can tell everyone, and they will know."

The man named Legion still wore his disposable facemask, which looked like it needed replacement. Well, Rhoda used her contacts to obtain a coronavirus vaccine a while ago, so she wasn't worried about infection. What did worry her was Legion had helter-skelter eyes under the third-degree lighting basement.

"Look-it, I'm a reporter. I try and dig out information from people. Thus, I bug them, ply them with alcohol, bullshit them sometimes, whatever it takes to get the facts. Then I publish a story with Northwest News. Next, I go to the next lead—"

Rhoda screamed as Legion hit her with a stun gun.

"Liar!" Legion shouted. "You and all the other news people, the ones on television, radio, in newspapers, you are paid to vomit out what the government says is true. Or to make money. 1984 has been with us for years. Look at all the lies about the virus from Wuhan. And the vaccine is worthless."

"Look, Legion. Tell me your story. I'll get it in print—"

Rhoda screamed again as Legion shocked her again. She jerked and kicked and tried to free herself from the padded handcuffs, which were higher quality than they looked. The man ripped her blouse open, yanked her bra off her substantial breasts. Then he applied the stun gun to her nipples.

"Scream all you want, bitch. No one will hear you in my basement," sneered the man self-named Legion. "I inherited this house from my mother. She died in a nursing home after getting the Coronavirus vaccine. Lot of good it did her."

The man stopped his abuse for a few minutes, and Rhoda tried to regain her voice. "Why... why are you doing this? I did nothing to you."

"You and your kind—one minute you tell us things are okay, the next minute we are fucked. You so-called news people use fear and joy to manipulate us."

Legion started to pull her pants down. She tried to twist and turn to make it more difficult as she knew where he was planning on applying the stun gun next.

"Quit fighting me or I'll do worst."

"Please. I'll tell your story. I'll tell the truth."

"Oh, so now you want to tell the truth," sneered the man. "Let's play some more, then maybe we'll talk."

A figure leapt from the bottom of the basement stairs. Legion noticed it a second too late.

"You—"

An extreme high kick cut off the rest of the abuser's comment. Legion's snapped back, and he fell backward to the basement cement floor. As Rhoda's eyes focused, she saw who the kicker was.

"You—Kupar. How did you—"

A male appeared who Rhoda recognized as Agent Richard Johnson. "You must be a good landlord, Rhoda Roberson," he said. "Your tenant in the other half of the duplex called in your possible abduction and got Mr. Roskin's car license plate. We were able to put a track and trace on your cellphone also."

"The fact we had a BOLO on you since you kept following us helped get the word to us quick," added Kim. "We took the lead and beat others here."

Kim freed Rhoda from the restraints. "We'll call for an aid car."

"Let me stomp on his nuts first."

"Can't allow that. Sorry."

"How'd you get into the house?"

"Creative lock picking," said Richard. "Exigent circumstances. If you hold your ears to the door lock hole, you could just hear your screams."

"What happens to—Roskin is his name?"

"He'll be locked up for a long, long time. Either in a place for the criminally insane or a maximum-security prison. This guy is a complete sadistic nutjob."

Perry Jones ordered Rhoda to take time off. She refused until she wrote The Story. Even though Rhoda violated a primary tenant of old-time reporting by becoming the story rather than just reporting it, the national media picked up her story and beat it to death. Soon, talking heads wanted to interview her. Rhoda tried not to tell all about where the asshat used the taser as some things should be kept private about her private parts. She kept her word about writing the truth, investigated David Roskin's mother's death. And she put in a whole bunch of digs into her profession about promoting fear and division for ratings and advertising dollars. After all, most politicians used what was on the airwaves to shape public opinion and get re-elected. If It Bleeds, It Leads and brings in campaign contributions.

Rhoda was even invited back as a sometimes-paid lecturer at her old Alma Mater. Then, of course, there were requests for dinner dates.

"Fame sucks," Rhoda grumbled at her desk.

"Hey Rhoda," asked Perry Jones, "you going to get all swell-headed and leave us when you win that Pulitzer Prize?"

"What, and give up all this? Not a chance."

Besides, she thought, *think of all those stories from the Why Files I just know are out there. After all, just the facts, ma'am.*

"Hey, Perry. About a trip to Port Angeles… there are reports of a loose Bengal tiger."

Her boss groaned and wished DC Comics never invented Lois Lane.

FILE 6
PASSION & PUSSYCATS

Diana Carnegie was not your stereotypical cat lady. She was not some aging spinster, frustrated divorcee, or a woman hiding from reality. She was a widow, but quite a young one at that. Diana was also quite well off financially and could justify being called 'rich.'

Her late husband, David Carnegie, was quite successful in real estate. He had also invested well in the stock market, including pharmaceuticals.

Then David, barely thirty and about to start with a family with his younger wife Diana, was hit by an Uber Eats delivery vehicle.

Did someone mention that David also had a million-dollar life insurance policy?

Diana was quite well-educated and was finishing a Master's in Business Administration when she married David after a whirlwind romance. Not everyone in the family was happy as Diana came from a middle class, not an upper class. Diana ignored the glares and snippy remarks. She loved David, and he loved her. So, fuck them.

When the delivery driver killed David, Diana ensured her husband had a nice but not ostentatious funeral. Against his family's wishes, she had him cremated as David had never stipulated what to do with his remains. David had severe allergies to animals, so any thought of donating organs to anyone was out of the question as Diana believed such things could be passed on to others.

However, as much as she loved David, his allergies were a sore spot in their marriage. Diana always had pets in her childhood. After his funeral, Diana set the urn with his ashes on the massive oak antique dining table and drove to the local animal shelter.

Diana sold the Jaguar and BMW soon after David's death. She had demanded cash and placed the proceeds in the home safe. Diana wanted some quick currency around the house, so the widow did not have to dip into the insurance or investment monies. She purchased an older SUV that its previous owner rarely used. This 4x4 was the vehicle she drove to the animal shelter.

The feline gods must have been guiding her that day as someone had dumped a litter of just weaned kittens on the back steps of the facility. When the attractive blonde Diana flashed a wad of bills and said she would take all six kittens, the shelter staff asked few questions. They were ecstatic when she dropped a couple of C-notes for the shelter workers to use for themselves, 'off the books' was her phrasing. A private condition was she left them her new business card for the Carnegie Local Animal Welfare and the admonition to call her if they had any dumped animals who needed a good home.

Diana went straight to a local pet store, dropped a thousand dollars on pet care products, food and toys. The rich woman also hired a college student working her way towards a veterinary degree. The student, Judith Wells, readily accepted the offer of moving into the large mansion and estate. Diana let the regular estate staff go with a generous bonus with the suggestion Diana was to sell the estate soon. In reality, Diana had other plans.

"Judith, I will pay for your schooling and pay off your student debt if you stay here and help me in my endeavor."

"Which is what?" the brunette student asked.

"I plan on creating a nonprofit animal welfare organization. I find I enjoy the company of God's creatures so much more than humans. My in-laws cemented that opinion in my mind." Diana smiled at Judith. "Present company excepted. I get some good vibrations from you."

"Thank you. I'll make sure I don't disappoint you."

"Finish your studies and then you can work full-time for me as the on-site vet. Until you decide to marry and have a family, of course."

"No plans for that anytime soon, Mrs. Carnegie."

"Please, call me Diana. Now, let me show you your suite."

Diana and Judith spent the rest of the day modifying a recreation room for the kittens. They paused and looked on with satisfaction at their creation.

"There is enough space for the cats to grow into," said Diana. "Once they're a bit older, they will be able to roam outside. That is, after I put a cat-proof fence up."

Judith laughed. "Good luck discovering that, Diana. Felines are natural climbers."

"I have some original designs. But come, let's have dinner with a glass of good wine. I'm hungry."

Diana surprised her new assistant with her cooking abilities. The two ladies finished off some sauteed salmon, a crisp salad and fresh strawberries in an hour.

"When do you have to go back to class, Judith?"

"Day after tomorrow. I will need to move out of my dorm room."

"I'll use the SUV and help."

Judith sipped her wine and then set it down. "I feel like I am taking advantage of you, Diana. And I also have this fear the next shoe will drop."

Diana refilled their glasses as she answered. "Of course you do. This rich young widow pops up out of nowhere and asks you to move into her mansion. She says she will pay all your education bills so you can be her veterinarian for a bunch of stray and rescued animals. Of course, you wonder if there is a major catch."

"Well, Diana. Is there?"

The blonde laughed. "There is a small one—no sleepovers with some hunk. No loud drunken parties. And you must sleep here other than if there is a family emergency—in case the animals need you."

"Well, those aren't any big deals. I hope you don't shock easily, but guys do nothing for me in the libido department. Been there, done that."

"Then, a toast, young lady," said Diana. The two ladies smiled and clinked glasses.

"Now, let's make sure the kittens are okay for the night. I'll get you some towels for the shower in your suite and I think I have some pajamas which will fit you. We are very similar in size."

"You sure you want me to stay the night, not just meet me in the morning at my dorm room?"

"Why? I said I would drive you in the morning and help you move. No strings attached other than I plan to work you to death with the animals."

Judith laughed and raised her glass in salute. "Okay. Sold."

A couple of hours later, the kittens were zonked out together in a padded pet's bed. Judith went up to her new room—more like a suite—took a long and luxurious hot shower, and washed her hair. She stepped out and began to dry herself off. There was a soft knock at the suite door. Judith wrapped a fluffy towel around her body with its curves and bumps in all the right places.

"Yes, Mistress—" Judith's humorous quip froze as she saw Diana standing wrapped up in a matching towel fresh from her shower.

"Remember what I said about getting good vibrations?" Diana asked with a half-smile.

"Yes," Judith replied, open appreciation on her face. "And you were right."

The younger—by just a few years—brunette reached

across and playfully yanked Diana's towel off. Diana giggled and repaid the favor. "We *are* the same size," the rich girl said.

Judith took in all of Diana, saying only, "Mm... yes."

Diana saw the desire on Judith's face and asked her simply, "Come to bed?"

Two nude, half-wet bodies became entwined on the queen-sized bed.

Diana moved Judith into the mansion in record time. Some cash crossed into specific hands to ensure Judith had no difficulties in changing addresses and guarantee her continued studies. The wealthy benefactor even arranged for Judith to receive extra school credit for her work at CLAW.

The litter of kittens soon grew like bad weeds. Diana found homes for four of them and kept two while taking on additional orphans. They thought about a watchdog or two but decided on a robotic one instead. Diana had stock in a tech company that gave her a four-legged robot Doggie they were developing as a test machine. The fact it was free was a definite selling point. The year flew by with Judith being at the top of her class at the college.

"A steady home and love life make all the difference," said Judith as she spanked Diana's nude ass. Just then, the front gate bell rang.

"Are we expecting a delivery?" asked Diana.

"Not that I know. I'll go check," Judith told her.

Diana went to the kitchen for a cold drink. When Judith didn't come back, Diana went looking for her. She met the brunette at the front door as Judith walked up the driveway from the main gate. The student vet had a large box in her arms.

"Delivery?" asked Diana.

"More like a drive-by. Look what's in the box."

A larger than usual kitten looked up at Diana as she peeked inside. The feline immediately tried to jump out. It took both of the women to keep it in the box. The sizeable young cat wanted out bad, spitting and trying to force its way out.

After they were inside with the box, Diana and Judith shut the front door and let the kitten escape. It didn't go far, not hiding like many a kitten in new surroundings. Instead, it stopped a few feet away, turned and looked at the two women with a steady gaze of a predator.

"What do we have here?" asked Diana.

"Some species with long fangs. Those do not look like normal kitten teeth," said Judith.

"Well, let's see if we can get it to a cage or into the spare room until he or she gets used to the new surroundings."

Some soft cat food was all that was required to bring the tawny feline with subdued stripes to heel. Judith quickly ascertained it was an unfixed tomcat.

"He's not a real young kitten. He's weaned." Judith said.

"He is big and stocky. But he is not some bobcat or lynx kitten someone grabbed by accident, either," added Diana.

"So, tomorrow we introduce him to the others. I'll get an electronic collar for him and we'll put him in the spare cat room."

The two women prepared a litterbox for him and watched as he quickly made use of it.

"Hmm. Diana, he has spent time in captivity."

"Yes. And some asshole dumped this cat after he looked like he would be this considerable-sized feline."

"Name?" asked Judith.

"Hmm. Baron? He has a regal air about him."

"Baron, you like that name?" asked Judith. The substantial feline walked up, rubbed against the two humans, and purred.

"He is quite the ladies' man," said Diana.

The two women fussed a bit with him, scratched his ears and then took him to the spare room they used for new arrivals. They found a couple of new cat toys for him, then left him alone.

"Hopefully, he'll be tired out," said Diana.

"Yes, and speaking of tired, shall we continue our playtime?"

Diana answered with a slight slap to Judith's cheek.

The added excitement of the new feline seemed to add passion to their lovemaking.

"Think this will ever get old?" asked Diana.

"Never. I love you, Diana. Our bodies fit together."

"We do make a sexy couple, Judith."

"Can I ask a question?" said Judith.

"Go ahead. I thought I'd shared almost everything with you."

"Why did you marry a man when you like women so much?"

"Well, because I like men, too. I did truly love David. I didn't marry him for his money nor push him in front of that car. Why do you ask after all this time?"

"Took me this long to get the courage up. I didn't want to make you angry."

Diana leaned over and kissed her partner. "I could never really be mad at you. You are my soulmate. We can have a formal wedding after you graduate."

Judith blinked back some tears. "I never want to lose you."

"Never," Diana whispered.

A furry beast suddenly jumped up on the bed. Both women cried out and Diana yelled "Lights!" so they could see what had interrupted the private moment.

It was a purring Baron.

"I shut the door, Diana. I know I did."

"You didn't lock it?" asked Diana.

"Why? Never had to before."

Baron was a loud purring machine as he bumped his head into the two ladies and demanded ear scratches and pets.

"I think we should have named you Houdini," said Judith. "He must know how to use door latches and knobs."

"Well, no harm. I guess Baron wants to sleep with his two mommies."

"So, this one is not up for adoption," stated Judith.

"No. I think he just adopted us."

In the morning, Diana and Judith introduced him to the other half dozen cats. A couple of dozen felines had passed through the Carnegie Local Animal Welfare facilities, as well as two dogs, a horse, and a kangaroo. Local shelters knew that if they were overfull or had a particular case (like the kangaroo), CLAW would take the animals off their hands. However, felines of all types were Diana's passion. The widow spent time and funds remodeling the Feline House at the local Woodland Park Zoo and lobbied against illegal animal smuggling and breeding. She soon met local Fish and Wildlife Agents, Homeland Security Agents, and Washington State Wildlife officers.

Despite not being an adult cat, Baron soon let the other felines know who the boss was. One tomcat tried to disagree in the first week and learned the hard way. A few days later, Diana found a new home for the tomcat.

"Baron is growing so fast, he could seriously hurt the other male," said Judith.

"Figured out what he is?" asked Diana.

"No. I'll take a fresh blood and saliva sample for a DNA check. I've been delaying it. I'm afraid he could be a Frankenstein, one of those poor animals some illegal exotic animal breeder created. Then, we may have to turn him in to the authorities."

"I think I could pull some strings, Judith."

"Well, I hope so. Let me talk to a friend at the Zoo, see

if we can do it on the sly."

Three weeks later, as Baron grew larger, Judith obtained some results. "Baron is part big cat, probably tiger. Then someone really screwed with his DNA. I didn't push for any more results as my contact is nervous."

"We can keep him?"

"Yes, we can. My friend sat on the information. She has the hots for me."

Diana frowned at Judith. "Nobody is expecting some tickle and pinch under the sheets…"

"Honey, she may fantasize about it, but she knows I am spoken for."

Diana went ahead and added some additional security fencing along the brick wall and made sure Baron had an electronic collar connected to the security fence. If Baron tried to climb over it, he would get a shock and also be tracked. Once a month, a small work crew came in to clean the house (though not the cat or animal area) and take care of the grounds. Other than those people, Diana and Judith were private. No big parties and only attending social gatherings to keep their political and animal welfare contacts current. They worked at helping more unfortunate creatures and loved each other. Judith kept in touch with her family, but nobody visited which was excellent for Diana and Judith.

One day the two heard an odd crunching then mechanical squealing.

"What is that?" asked Judith. The two hurried out to the back expanse.

They soon saw the source of the sounds. Baron had the robot dog down and was tearing it apart. The now large cat finally had enough of the security robot following him.

"Baron! Bad kitty!" Diana's angry voice made Baron flatten his ears back as he stared at the two-legged mommies.

"Come here, you naughty boy," Judith said with a laugh. Baron then, as many a house cat did with a mouse, brought a bit of his trophy kill up and dropped it at the women's feet.

"What am I going to tell the corporation that gave me the robot to test?" asked Diana.

"They need to make a tougher product?"

The couple received a notice in their mailbox that local cats and dogs were disappearing.

"I don't think we have to worry with Baron around. He protects the remaining cats like his brood," Judith said.

Diana bit her lip and frowned. "You don't think it is Baron?"

"How does he get out, Diana? We'd know."

"I hope so. Baron is huge now. Luckily this estate has high shrubs, walls, fences, and lots of lands. We feed him, but he has hunting instincts."

"Tell you what. I'll set up a camera or two, Diana, just to be safe."

Diana hugged her lover. "Thanks. With us planning a wedding next month, I don't want anything to go wrong."

Two nights later, the women received an unfortunate bit of information.

"God, how did he do that?"

In the video, Baron leapt from an apple tree up to the top of the wall and then over the fence. He ignored the shock collar.

"That collar should have zapped him with a nasty jolt," said Judith. "I set it to the maximum."

"We'll have to double lock all the doors and make sure he stays in at night," answered Diana.

That night, Baron checked all the doors and windows, growled, then came to their bedroom and plunked down between them.

"God, you are big!" exclaimed Diana.

"You know, he has the size of a tiger but the disposition of a house cat," said Judith

"Those fangs are turning into butcher knives. Lucky, he thinks of us as his mommies."

Baron kept batting at them until they both scratched his ears.

"Okay, you big baby. You can sleep with us," said Diana. "I like pussy, but not this large."

Early that morning, Baron went to his oversized litter box to do his cat business. As he did, the front door slowly opened.

"I told you I had the security system keys and codes," one male voice said in a whisper.

"No dogs?" Another voice asked.

"Just that robot dog. But it was nowhere to be found."

"Come on," whispered a female. "The rich bitches

room is up those stairs."

"Yeah," whispered a second female voice. "Time for a tip for cleaning all their shit."

The four miscreants slowly ascended the stairs. They did not realize a set of predator's eyes followed them. The two men and two women burst into the master bedroom with the leader Evan yelling orders to the rudely awaken couple.

"Freeze, bitches! Time to pay the piper." Evan pointed a slab-sided automatic pistol at the women.

Diana recognized the scraggly bearded Evan as one of the men who helped install the virtual fence for Baron and the other animals.

"Is this how you repay clients?" Diana snapped at them. The blonde named Joan, a former housekeeper of Diana and Judith, came up to the bed holding a truncheon.

"Shut up, or I'll mess up your looks."

"What do you want?" Judith asked as she sized up the four. She was not going to go down without a fight.

"The money in the safe," said dark-haired Mary. Her meth addiction kept her much too thin.

"And your jewelry you rich cows wear," said Larry, the chubby male fourth member of the robbery group.

"Fuck you!" blurted Judith. Joan smacked Diana's shapely shoulder with the truncheon, and the blonde screamed in pain.

"Keep up the smart mouth and your girlfriend will be spitting teeth," said Joan with a feral grin.

"No one has to get hurt," said Evan.

"Oh, sure. You're going to let us live when we know

who you are," said Judith.

Larry pulled a butcher knife from his belt. "I think they need some persuasion."

An earsplitting roar froze all six humans. Baron leapt into the bedroom and bowled over Evan before he could use the pistol.

Mary screamed.

"What the hell is that?" demanded Joan

"Meet Baron, the man of the house," hissed Diana.

Baron's tail flicked like many a cat when it watched future prey or cat toys. Evan tried to grab his pistol from the carpeted floor and Baron pounced. A rodent had moved. The tiger cat opened its wide jaws and sank the fangs that Diana suddenly realized were like twin sabers into Evan's skull, shutting off a scream.

As crunching sounds filled the bedroom, the other three would-be robbers dashed towards the door. Mary and Joan ran into each other, tripped and both fell. Larry made it through the doorway and the top of the stairway. His footing slipped and he fell partway down the stairs, the butcher knife forgotten.

Joan and Mary tried to scramble past the big feline and were met with massive paw swipes. They bounced off the bedroom wall, and Baron leapt on both. Then he heard Larry on the stairs and realized one prey was escaping.

Baron bounded off the two stunned women and made a beeline to Larry. The chubby man regained his footing on the stairs just as Baron reached the top. Larry saw him, screamed like a little girl, and tried to flee down the stairs. A playful tiger cat leapt from the top of the stairway and down to the landing. Larry tried to stop his flight but ran into Baron. A massive paw smashed him across the landing and into the edge of the stairway railing.

Baron had yet to use his claws. He had been batting the prey with his paws as a housecat would play with a catnip mouse toy. When Larry screamed and tried to climb back up the stairs on all fours, Baron tested his claws' sharpness. Larry's back looked like a piece of butchered beef after just one swipe of a paw. Larry's screaming seemed to annoy Baron as the next blow broke his neck, silencing the man forever. Baron nudged the human body as if to start the chase again, then looked up the stairs. He heard one of the women he had knocked into the wall wail. Baron bounded up the stairway.

"Please, let us go," said Joan. "We'll just leave—"

A clawed swipe that removed the woman's bottom jaw cut off the rest of the plea. Blood splattered over the room and Mary. The skinny woman screamed and ran to the room's balcony. Baron let the prey reach the bedroom balcony before he moved. Mary grabbed some rosebush lattice and tried to climb down to the first floor. Baron watched from the edge of the terrace with a twitching tail.

"Baron," said Diana, "come here. Your mommies want you."

Both Diana and Judith slowly approached the creature of destruction. When Judith reached out to touch his flank, Baron turned his head and roared loud enough to match a T-rex in a movie. The hunting cat did not want to be disturbed.

"My God. What have we raised?" said Judith.

Mary reached the first level and sprinted out into the backyard. Baron leapt from the balcony and down to the ground. Mary was a fast runner, especially for a meth-head. But she was no match for this tiger cat. Baron crushed her to the lawn, then sank his saber teeth into her neck, twisted his jaws, and decapitated her. Baron next began batting her head around like a ball.

The two women had to call the police; they had no choice. They told dispatch a large tiger was involved. Thus, Diana was somewhat surprised but not wholly when DHS/HSI Special Agent Kim Kupar and federal Fish and Wildlife Agent Brenna Freiberg appeared along with the local Swat Team.

"Is that a capture rifle?" asked Diana.

"Yes, Diana," replied Kim. "Knowing you and CLAW, we hope to take the big cat alive."

"We wished you had called us before," said Brenna as she loaded the capture rifle. "You know us both. We would have helped you out."

"He's our boy," said Judith. "We are his two-legged mommies..." Her voice broke as she began to sob. Diana hugged her as she looked at the two agents, the SWAT team standing back geared up.

"My husband, Hank Thomas, got wind yesterday at the zoo that something was going on," said Kim. "The young zoo employee couldn't keep the DNA sample secret forever."

Diana and Judith looked at the slender East Indian and Argentine woman, with her Nordic shieldmaiden partner Brenna providing a study in contrasts. At least the women knew Baron and he would not be put down unnecessarily. Diana swallowed a lump in her throat.

"Can I try to get Baron to come?"

"We're still going to have to sedate him," said Brenna.

Diana and Judith both nodded and then slowly walked out to the back forty as Diana called it.

Baron was still playing with Mary's head. When he heard his two-legged mommies call, he came this time. The capture dart hit him in the side; he roared, managed to pull it out. The sedative injected and Baron soon staggered and fell over. Judith, as a trained vet, checked his breathing and pulse.

"I had to give him a little extra sedative," said Brenna.

"He can handle it. He is a big boy."

"We think he is one of Sir Khan's offspring," said Kim. "He has cougar genes in him, but the modified sabretooth cat DNA won out."

"Somebody took him from the Olympic National Forest?" asked Diana.

"Yes. You are lucky Sir Khan didn't come looking for him. He is astute and possessive."

Zoo staff helped load the big cat into a large cage then into the back of a truck.

"We can visit him?" asked Judith.

Brenna sighed. "If a judge doesn't order us to put him down. He did kill four humans. The fact he was doing it while protecting you two from armed burglars will be in his favor."

"Aw, fuck," said Diana and began to cry.

Diana finished a proposal for funding to some various benefactors in the mansion's study. She was still the Cat Lady in charge of CLAW. Judith burst into the room.

"Kim Kupar's on the phone. You gotta hear this."

"Yes, Kim. What's up?"

"Baron did a jailbreak. And he had help."

Baron followed his sire as they worked through the neighborhoods around the Woodland Park Zoo. A semi-tractor-trailer made an early morning delivery and Sir Khan led his son into the back and then concealed themselves behind some boxes. The driver was tired and running on caffeine, so he did not notice something had crawled into the end of the trailer.

The next stop was the Port of Tacoma. Two oversized shapes knocked the driver unconscious as the sabretooth cats fled. Normal big cats, even social lions, did not have the protectiveness towards older offspring. Senior males are usually chased out of a pride by young males once they reached an age to challenge the alpha.

Sir Khan and his offspring were not normal. He had caught the old scent of a particular female human at the Zoo when he had gone there looking for Baron. Sir Khan tracked his offspring for months; his additional intelligence gave him a single-mindedness no human would believe—except for the Tiger Lady.

Across the Tacoma Narrows Bridge in the middle of the night and Sir Khan was in familiar territory—the Kitsap

Peninsula, connected by a small stretch of land on the southeastern corner of the Olympic Peninsula. Soon the two cats would be in the Olympic National Forest. There, in Sir Khan's land, he would help his kind to survive and thrive. Soon, there would be an actual breeding population of a new apex predator.

John Wang and the other humans made one critical error when they created Sir Khan: They made him too bright, much too intelligent. As Sir Khan found other mates, natural selection would pass on the intelligence as a predator. Some of Sir Khan's creators would someday regret it.

FILE 7
COLD FEET

Kim Kupar looked in the full-length mirror at the bridal shop. The federal special agent wanted a tight-fitting Asian-inspired look in her gown for this special day. In her mind, it would be a once-in-a-lifetime experience. The idea of a second marriage was unthinkable. Hank Thomas was her one true love, and Kim planned to be married for the rest of the couple's natural lifespans.

She and Hank performed a civil ceremony to make them an official married couple earlier. The two lovers did that, as Kim's and Hank's involvement in the Why Files Project put them at risk. Being married meant additional health, life and survivor's insurance. Law enforcement was not always safe. Now, to keep Kim's family happy, they were about to have a 'real' wedding, followed by a real honeymoon.

The bridal gown she had selected seemed to fit the bill. Kim smiled at her image in the mirror.

"Your groom will have eyes only for you in this dress," the young clerk said with a smile. "It fits you as if it is made only for you."

"I know Hank only has eyes for me already. A bridal gown will not add to his love." Kim turned around once more, looking in the multiple-angle mirror. "If I want a few alterations, can you make them here?"

"Why, of course," replied the saleslady. "We have access to trained tailors and dressmakers."

Kim knew that once her Argentine mother saw the gown, she would have to add her two cents worth. Kim's mother had a good eye for fashion, so her suggestions were not all bad. Her Punjabi father just cared that she married a good man so that a clean gunny sack might suffice.

"Please let me put a deposit down to hold this gown until I can get my mother in here to see how it fits."

"But of course," said another voice—male, in accentless English.

"Excuse me?" Kim began a reply to the sudden shock of a male being in the female dressing room. Then a large hand pressed a thick cloth on her mouth. Kim lashed out with martial arts elbows and kicks as she realized the cloth over her mouth was soaked in some chemical. The HSI special agent saw the reflections of two huge men in the fitting room mirror as two sets of solid arms restrained her. Then things went black.

Kim was unsure as to the passage of time when she groggily regained consciousness. It took a few moments to realize she was in the back of a vehicle with some hood over her head. When the agent tried to move, Kim discovered someone had taped her hands and feet together.

Kim felt a seat belt restraint on her stomach as she tried to shift in her seat. No one had taped her mouth shut, so she called out.

"You realize you just kidnapped a federal law enforcement officer, don't you?"

"Ah, Kim Kupar. You are awake," the same voice from the bridal shop said. "Of course, we know who you are. This situation is not some random act by some perverts."

"Then, who are you? And where are you taking me?"

"Here, young lady. Let me remove your hood. I want you to know who I am."

Kim blinked her eyes for focus as the man removed the hood. Someone turned on a small interior and Kim looked at a Chinese face that seemed oddly familiar.

"I can tell your mind is working, Kim. Yes, I look familiar... as I am James Wang, brother of the late John Wang."

Kim's stomach sank. After all these months since John Wang's death, her former lover's family and criminal organization now chose to act and seek revenge? Kim knew she was, as the saying goes, in deep kimchee. "What do you want, Mister Wang?"

"Please, call me James. After all, we were almost related by marriage. The gown you are wearing should have been for your and John's wedding."

"You know why that was impossible, James."

James smiled. "You know enough money and power can fix most anything, Kim. You could have given the situation a chance."

"You have not answered all of my questions. What do you want, and where are we going?"

"Why, primarily my family and the organization in mainland China want revenge. You cost us a fine man as well as millions in revenue. But we also have a secondary desire."

"What is that?"

"Sir Khan. We need to recover that unique property."

Kim knew that James Wang and his conspirators must know of the unique relationship the created sabretooth cat had with the Special Agent. Kim could imagine how much they may have learned about the Why Files by cyber-hacking, something in which the Chinese communist government had profound expertise. Not to mention the information gleaned from open-source platforms.

"So then, James, where are you taking me?"

"An interesting question, Kim Kupar." Wang shifted in the seat opposite Kim as he smiled more. "The original plan was a slow boat to Vancouver, British Columbia and an area often called Little Hong Kong. Many Chinese immigrated to Canada when Great Britain allowed Hong Kong to revert to China. There you would be tortured both for revenge and information on your investigative activities."

Kim knew James's loose lips meant the plan was to eliminate her when they finished their revenge. The man had a similar narcissistic ego to John. Kim realized she would have to observe for a chance to escape.

"But your plans changed," said Kim.

"Very mindful of you, Kim. I suggested we use you to lure Sir Khan back for capture, then have fun with you. Sir

Khan is unique and expensive."

"And if it doesn't work?"

"Then, my jade-eyed beauty, back to Plan One."

"So, we are traveling to the Olympic National Forest near Port Angeles."

"Yes, Kim. We have done our homework and know the territory Sir Khan claims as his own."

The vehicle was a former utility van with no windows in the rear, so James decided to leave off Kim's hood. Besides Wang, Kim counted the driver and two other henchmen in the vehicle. He saw the driver talking on a small radio, so she assumed there was at least one other vehicle traveling with them. Kim reasoned they did not take the chance of a ferry ride with more prying eyes and drove around over the Tacoma Narrows Bridge to the Peninsula. Kim was unsure as to how long she had been unconscious from the chloroform. Kim sat silently and did some time measurement by counting in her head the seconds. As time passed, Kim thought she felt the familiar passage over the Hood Canal bridge and knew they were an hour or so from Sir Khan's claimed territory.

Kim knew the night was approaching as the sunlight through the front vehicle windows was reduced. She knew trying to contact Sir Khan in darkness was far from safe. However, the Chinese operatives seemed confident in their ability to use the night hours for concealment while catching a large feline.

"May I have some water?" Kim asked.

"But of course, my jade beauty," James Wang answered and quickly produced a water bottle. As Kim's hands were bound, he helped her drink from the plastic bottle. James smile as he set it down.

"John and I had many conversations about you. He *was* in love with you, to the extreme. I tried to talk him out of continuing a relationship once he realized our organization was under investigation." James sighed. "I told him such love might cost him his life. And then you killed him."

"I did not kill him. His creation Sir Khan did."

"However, his love for you led to the—final act. So, you are ultimately responsible."

James paused, seemed to examine her closely. "My brother told me about your lovemaking. The way he talked about it made me see you as a succubus. Sitting next to you, in the flesh... I can see how your erotic and exotic nature could captivate even my brother." James cocked his head to one side and then the other, observing her from different angles. "Your Argentine and East Indian ancestry seem to have created a rare beauty. Perhaps I can convince the *powers-that-be* and my family elders to keep you on as a concubine. To torture and then kill you seems like such a waste."

Kim tried not to show her anger at the suggestion. "You realize I am to be married in a few days."

"Do you love this man, this Hank Thomas, as much as your professed love for John?"

"What do you think?" Kim replied. She hoped James was exaggerating the 'research' into her life but now realized he had not. She wondered just how long they had been watching her, digging into every nook and cranny of her life. Kim admitted she should just ask and keep James talking.

"When did you and your comrades start planning this kidnapping?"

"A plan for revenge began days after John's untimely death. The other Japanese Yakuza wanted to send a modern-day ninja to butcher you, your brother, his wife Jade, Rex Moyer, and his family. They were quite angry that Mr. Yoshida died in such a manner. He held a high position in their organization."

"But you and yours convinced them otherwise," said Kim.

"Yes. I, in fact, completed the negotiations. As the aggrieved member of John's family, his closest brother, they respected my opinions more than any normal negotiator. Thus, I convinced them that revenge is a meal best served at leisure so that one may savor all its flavors."

"That is a rather poetic way of saying you would kill me and mine as payback."

James laughed. "Payback seems a rather crass description of the situation," said the Chinese Triad member. "I like the image of a blood feud. One that may continue past you until the lust for revenge is satiated."

"The more people you kill, the more people will hunt you."

James grinned as he spoke. "Once the authorities realize the true nature of the deaths, yes. But we have ways to delay that realization." James leaned in and gently stroked her face. Kim concentrated on not jerking away. If she was to survive, the fantasy of being his concubine must be an option, at least in James' mind.

"You know how easy it is, my jade-eyed beauty, to create a note in your handwriting that you have—how do you say it—a case of cold feet about marriage? That you need a few days alone?"

"Hank would not believe you. Neither would my father and mother."

"A voice mail in your voice would add to the story. We Chinese are quite good at data and electronic manipulation." James seemed to wave away any possible protests.

"But maybe I can convince certain people to be less—demanding, shall we say if Sir Khan is returned to us. He is such a unique and valuable creature. This sabretooth cat is a prime example of my organization's skill in genetic manipulation."

Kim saw James had inherited the same smoothness of his dead brother, John. However, Kim learned from her mistakes that the smoothness was a form of sociopathic behavior. The agent also knew that her options were limited and the longer she kept him engaged in a personal discussion, the better chance for her survival.

Kim noticed dusk arrived through the front windshield. The night in the woods could conceal many crimes; Kim hoped reduced light might offer her a chance at escape. The special agent thought she saw city street lights through the windshield and believed they were driving through Port Angeles. A few glimpses of traffic signals confirmed her suspicions.

"It will not be long now, Kim. Hopefully, Sir Khan will soon reunite with you. And thus, we will once again have him in custody."

Kim soon realized they were traveling along Highway 101 on the north edge of the Olympic National Park and the Olympic National Forest. She had a sinking feeling in her stomach when the driver turned off the paved road surface and onto an unimproved roadway. Kim could bet where they were taking her. The vehicles would soon be some fifteen miles northeast of Forks in the Olympic National Forest and ten miles from the border with the Olympic National Park.

"You're taking me to a particular location. Two forest service officers died there at an unauthorized cabin since torn down. Some Russians had a nearby breeding experiment similar to Sir Khan."

"My brother always said you were too astute for your own good," James Wang said with a grin—which was almost a sneer.

"You realize the Park Rangers and U.S. Forest Officers patrol that location almost every day."

"Our lookouts report the last patrol was there an hour ago. It is nearing shift change for the federal officials, so we will have more than sufficient time to locate Sir Khan. And if an official stumbles on us—well, the forest can hide many a secret to include human remains."

"You may make me disappear while I am off duty, James. But on-duty personnel? Don't press your luck."

The Chinese organized crime figure shrugged and then replied, "We will cross that bridge when we get to it, is the American expression."

Kim noticed the driver slip the van into a four-wheel-drive mode and realized James left nothing to chance. The Triad official planned all of this action; she was sure of it.

"So, what is the plan once we are at the site of the former cabin?" Kim asked.

"Why, simplicity in its purest sense. You call out for Sir Khan and we wait. My research shows you and he have an almost psychic connection. If the huge feline is anywhere near the location, he will come."

"And if he shows up, then what?"

"*When* he shows up, I will demonstrate once we arrive at our destination."

A half-hour later, the van stopped. The two huge men quickly exited the van and opened the back doors. James helped them remove Kim from the bench seat and stood her up next to the rear right wheel. One of the men produced a knife and cut Kim's feet loose.

"If you run, we will hunt you down," James said with a smile.

Kim looked around. Yards in front of the dark-colored van, she saw the remains of the demolished cabin. This action was the play's second act that began in The Jade Palace nightclub's hidden basement. There John Wang had introduced Kim to Sir Khan. She was to be prey for the mutant feline. Instead, Sir Khan killed John and let Kim live.

Kim stood silent and watched as six other men from the trailing SUV removed equipment boxes and cases. Kim saw some unusual-looking long guns in two of the henchmen's hands as others placed some low light lanterns around the perimeter.

"Ah, you noticed some of our unique toys," said James. He called over in Mandarin, and one of the men brought a long gun to him. It looked to Kim like a modified assault shotgun. "This, my dear, is an extraordinary capture gun. It shoots a self-contained taser shell with enough electrical shock effect to knock down a full-grown horse. Each weapon holds four rounds." James grinned. "A Chinese invention."

"Well, if it works, how do you plan to keep Sir Khan? He will eventually wake up," said Kim.

James snapped his fingers and pointed. The two oversized Asian males who kidnapped Kim stepped over, holding a massive metallic capture net.

"Another Chinese design?" asked Kim.

"Why, of course. As are the two men who are holding it."

"What..." Then it dawned on Kim. They could have been the late Samu's siblings.

"You sick bastards. You're still screwing with the human genome. How old are they, fourteen like Samu?"

"Fifteen. A better version with no reduced intellect as in poor Samu's case." James sighed. "I am sad my brother died. But he made his bed, as the saying goes. However, I feel guilty about how loyal Samu died. He did what he was told and Sir Khan killed him for his efforts."

James Wang snapped some Mandarin orders and one of the men from the SUV talked on a small radio. The man then nodded at James, who smiled.

"Our lookouts are in place. They have been in the

forest for some forty-eight hours and will be glad when they can exit."

"But no joy on Sir Khan," Kim said.

"Some pug marks of a large feline, but no visuals yet."

"Ever think the sabretooth cat is smart enough to stay away?" Kim asked.

"Ah, but that is where you come in, my beauty. Please scream."

Kim glared at James Wang. "Go fuck yourself."

One of the overgrown Chinese men grabbed and squeezed Kim in her most sensitive areas. A scream of pain flew from her mouth before she could stop it.

"See, these two are well trained and capable of more than just feeding a beast," said James with a sneer.

The henchman elicited another scream from Kim before she stifled herself by biting her lip. The man let her fall to the earth.

"Hey, what's going on here?" a new voice asked.

Through teary eyes, Kim saw a scruffy-looking man who fit the stereotype image of 'homeless.' She started to yell out a warning when one of the gangsters stepped forward and shot a short crossbow pistol bolt through his throat. The unfortunate witness stumbled back gagging, then toppled over.

"There was no need for that!" Kim spat out.

"Yes, there was," replied Wang. "No witnesses and no interference of tonight's occurrences. We just demonstrated how we cross the bridge when it is necessary. And an arrow can be explained as a hunting accident, no telltale rifling like with bullets."

Kim prayed that there were no more homeless individuals or campers wandering around the forests this night. She knew James Wang was willing to have a stack of bodies if it kept his mission to recapture Sir Khan alive. The special agent managed to stand, swearing silently she would not cry out again, no matter the pain.

Wang frowned at her. "I am sorry I had to be so-forceful in obtaining the requested reaction on your part. But you would not call out voluntarily, would you, Agent Kupar?"

"No. And you will not get a similar response from me this evening."

James chuckled, "My brother said you had a wild fiery spirit. He said it reminded him of the wild American mustang. I should like to see one of these horses close up someday, not just in films."

A handheld radio crackled to life. James stepped over and talked in low tones with the radio operator. He returned, smiling to where Kim now stood.

"Night thermal vision has picked up a sizeable warm-bodied creature approaching from the south. It is coming up fast. I guess we will soon see Sir Khan in the flesh and this night's adventure may end earlier than planned."

James motioned to another of the Asian henchmen, and the man brought a large briefcase to his boss. James opened it and removed a large framed Glock semiautomatic pistol, in .45 or 10MM. The henchman took an MP-5K compact submachine gun from the same case.

"I thought you wanted to capture, not kill Sir Khan."

James shrugged. "Sometimes plans go astray, Kim. You know that. An unfortunate miscalculation killed a close friend of yours when an employee did not disarm a boobytrap as directed."

"Matt Swenson."

"That was his name? John never mentioned it."

The same level of non-empathetic psychopathy infected the Wang Family throughout if James and John were standard clan members. James talked about her former mentor Matt's death as if he were speaking of a goldfish's end in a home aquarium.

"You know he had a wife and children, James."

"That is unfortunate. Like John, he left loved ones behind."

"You know what I promised his wife, Pat?"

James gave her a quizzical look.

"James, I promised I would get the scum, the bastards that killed her husband. John was the first."

Kim could see even in the reduced light James' jaw tighten. She had hit a nerve.

"Maybe I will not promote your continued existence so vigorously," James coldly stated. "Maybe you need to be terminated with painful prejudice."

A radio squawked and then went silent. John walked over to the operator who was trying to raise the person who transmitted. After a minute of trying, James walked around the area and, using Mandarin, told the other personnel to keep alert.

"Plans changed?" Kim asked.

James stepped up and slapped her. "Shut up, half-breed twat."

A scream echoed from the forest, then cut off in mid cry. Kim watched another man produce a shotgun from the SUV as the security spread out. One minion had a night vision unit and surveyed the forest out past the low light lanterns' limited illumination. He excitedly pointed towards a patch of darkness and the men with the two specialized capture guns stepped forward and peered in that direction, weapons at ready.

A scream came from behind Kim and she managed to spin around in time to see something drag the van driver off into the darkness. A shot rang out, then another scream in the dark. James began to yell orders as someone jumped into the SUV and turned on the headlights. The vehicle light beams briefly lit a fast-moving figure passing through the illumination field. Then another scream echoed from off to Kim's right as a henchman fired a capture taser gun.

Kim laughed, then yelled in Mandarin, "Your research was shit, James. You did not notice Sir Khan also had African lion genes. He has a pack, a hunting pride! A fucking family!"

Kim dashed behind the transport van and tried to find a rough edge to use on her duct tape-bound hands; as she did, an all too familiar roar reverberated in the forest.

"Sir Khan," Kim whispered. Then James was next to her and pointed the Glock in her face.

"Call him off!" he demanded.

"If I could, why would I? I will be dead anyway."

"You—" James Wang never finished his comment. His

head disappeared in the maw of a sabretooth cat. The Glock discharged in the air and then Kim heard the crunching sounds of saber-shaped canines penetrating a human skull. She closed her eyes as there were certain things she did not want to see.

A minute later and it was over. Kim worked on her bound hands and somehow freed them. Behind her came a prominent feline cough. The Tiger Lady slowly turned around. Sir Khan's immense face came within inches from hers, and she felt his hot breath. Then, the mutated Bengal tiger purred as a large housecat and head-butted her for an ear scratch and a pet. She blinked back tears as she hugged and scratched him.

"What am I going to do with you, my furry friend?" Kim whispered. "You keep saving me, yet people want you in a cage."

From miles, away came the familiar *whop, whop, whop* of Blackhawk helicopter blades beating the air into submission. The late James Wang did not know Richard Johnson, the senior agent in the investigative group, arranged with the surveillance technician Kelly Olivet to surgically place some tracking devices in the team members. After the infamous problems with certain blue-skinned beings and holes in time and space, there was a need to track people for possible rescue. Kim now knew they worked.

"You need to make yourself scarce, my big fella. Even these friends of mine will want you in a zoo."

Kim looked into the night and saw several pairs of shiny feline eyes.

"'*Tiger Tiger burning bright, in the forests of the*

night,'" Kim quoted William Blake as she gave her special friend a parting pet. "You have a great-looking family. Keep them safe. Someday, my husband and I may have children of our own for you to meet."

A final head-butt, a cough, and Sir Khan was—*gone.* He and his pride were as ghosts. Hopefully, Sir Khan and his family had some caves to hide in away from human surveillance technology. Kim really did not want them in a zoo, poked and prodded by Men in Black and government scientists.

Kim Kupar found a flashlight and used it to flash S.O.S in the approaching helicopters' direction. She needed to get back; she had a wedding to do. And her wedding dress was ruined.

Weeks later, after her honeymoon, Kim sat in Assistant Special Agent in Charge Tim Weiss' office with Richard Johnson. Weiss sipped his coffee, then spoke.

"Kim, you know Sir Khan needs to be on game preserve or in some kind of high-end Zoo. He and his pride are making people nervous. Not to mention what will happen if an elk hunter crosses paths with them."

Kim sighed. "I know. But Sir Khan is so… free."

Weiss looked at Richard. "You two work it out. It has to be done. Sorry."

As the partners walked back to their offices, Richard looked at Kim. "Think you can help keep him hidden?" he asked.

"Maybe. Are you willing to stick your neck out

on this?"

"Hell, yes. That big cat saved yours and my butts. We owe Sir Khan."

Miles away, a brilliant feline led his pride into a series of hidden caverns in the Olympic Mountains. Once hinted at in hazy memories, the caverns were now unknown to even the indigenous people in the area.

Sir Khan sniffed the air. If this idea failed, he had scented land to the north across the saltwater sound. He would lead his pride across, stowing away on some cargo barge to reach Canada. Then, maybe what humans called Alaska.

Sir Khan coughed, then let out a short roar. For now, he was still boss, here. It was best no one forgot that fact—especially foolish monkeys.

FILE 8
LOVE IS BLUE

Chapter One

So, you say she just… appeared?" Senior Special Agent Richard Johnson asked as Special Agent Kim Kupar looked on. Sector Control called the two agents to investigate a bizarre report from the Homeland Security/Immigration and Customs Enforcement Detention Center in Seattle. When Sector Control notified them, it was about an unauthorized person inside the detention center.

Senior Detention Office Paco De La O had a confused and uncomfortable look on his face. He had made the call and now had this unlikely-looking duo in front of him. "Yes, Agent. We found the woman in a back interview room. No one remembers taking her there."

"There's no video of her before she appeared in the back room?" asked Kim Kupar.

"No, ma'am. There are some glitches, small spots of what seems to be interference on the video recordings. Then, she is there."

"Are you sure she is a she?" Kim asked.

"We sent a couple of female officers to search after we discovered her. They confirmed she is biologically female. Although the shade of her skin is a bit—odd?"

"How so?" asked Richard.

"It would be best if you saw for your selves."

"Let's take a look at the video recordings first," said Kim. "I want to see how long these glitches lasted."

Paco De La O took the two agents to the main video surveillance room. The numerous surveillance camera feeds eventually led to this control room. The on-duty technician replayed the various recordings from multiple angles of the detention center.

After watching the digital and tape recordings several times, Kim spoke. "There seems to be a two-second pause or interference on all these recordings at midnight. Then you see this stranger on the main camera covering the back interview room."

"The Witching Hour," said Richard.

"Which could be a coincidence. We'll have to check with Puget Sound Power to see if there was a power surge at that time."

Richard squinted at one of the video screens. "Hmmm. Let's look at this stranger close up. I want to see that skin hue close up."

Paco led them to the interview room. The two agents looked through the two-way mirrored glass at the person seated. The detection staff handcuffed one hand of the woman to a restraining ring built into the table frame.

"So, you saw her first here, in this room?" asked Kim.

"Yes, ma'am," answered De La O.

"Her skin does look bluish-gray or purple-like," Richard said.

"Well, let's go in and see if we can find a common language," said Kim.

"I tried Spanish," said the detention supervisor. "It didn't work."

The two special agents went into the locked room. The woman with the bluish skin impassively sat as she watched them enter. Kim smiled and tried a greeting in Mandarin Chinese. The woman shook her head in the universal negative. Kim attempted her native Punjabi, then bits of a couple of East Indian dialects, then some Japanese she had picked up over the years. The woman shook her head 'no' at all the greetings.

"Let's get her a pen and paper and see if she can write something in her language. We can do a computer matchup."

Kim made motions of drinking, and the woman nodded her head yes. Richard left and returned with a plastic bottle of water plus a pen and paper. Kim smiled as she laid the items in front of the unknown female. The woman unscrewed the cap on the water bottle and drank half of it, then set it down with a half-smile on her face. She then took up the pen and put it on the paper.

"Common items," said Richard.

"So, similar cultural aspects," replied Kim.

The woman held the paper steady with her handcuffed left hand while writing with her right. She was quick in her writing and drawing. Five minutes later, she pushed the form towards the agents.

Richard whistled. "Are those hieroglyphics?"

"They are very similar, to say the least, Richard. Unfortunately, I know no Egyptian and just a few symbols in ancient Sumerian. Her writing doesn't look like Chinese Hanzi or Japanese Kanji."

"Well, Kim, I guess we could start with 'Me Tarzan, you Jane' attempts at communication while we run these symbols and pictographs through a computer."

"Might as well. Then we get to figure out what to do with this woman. She looks about my size and age. I may be able to find some clothes for her while we take hers and try some forensic examinations on them to find her identity. I don't think it is actually fair to hold her in a cell when she does not even seem to know where she is right now."

"So, we have a five-foot-seven or thereabouts young lady with European features but bluish skin and dark hair. We can send her photo out to all the various Law Enforcement and Intelligence agencies. We may find a—"

The woman jerked her attention to the wall opposite the two-way mirror. She began to yell in some unknown language and a tall silvery figure seemed to pop through the wall. The woman screamed and tried to dodge a grasping hand.

Kim and Richard were both out of their chairs and reaching for weapons. Maybe because they had dealt with all manner of strange creatures, including flying dragons, they were not stunned into inaction by a being coming through a wall. Kim swung a collapsible baton at the grasping hand and broke its grip on the unknown woman. Richard had his pistol out as he hit the panic button and yelled at the being to halt.

A shiny blade slashed through the table at the point of attachment for the handcuffs. The woman screamed and lurched free. Richard fired his pistol at the bright being. Bullet impacts forced the being back as the women skittered around the two agents. The being came off the wall and missed Kim by a hairsbreadth with its blade, only her martial arts training saving her. She struck at the weapon holding arm with her baton but failed to knock the swordlike weapon from the creature's grasp.

Richard let out a war cry and emptied his pistol into the attacker's face and head. Sparks similar to a shorting toaster showered the room and the humanoid shape collapsed.

Kim looked up in time to see the blue-skinned woman slide through the creature's point of entry in the wall.

The ICE Detention Officers burst into the room in time to see the wall opening pop shut.

Hours later, the two agent partners shared alcoholic libations at a hole-in-the-wall establishment run by a former cop. He was more than willing to open it at irregular hours for an exclusive clientele.

"What just happened?" asked Kim.

"Well, we just received a visit from a no-name agency

who once again made us swear to secrecy."

"Before that, Richard."

"Another proof for string theory and the multiverse. Examination of that robot hunter thing will keep some Alphabet Organizations busy for months—if not years."

"You did a number on its head, Richard."

"Well, I can't let it hurt my partner, can I? Especially since you have a husband at home."

"You ever going to be married, Richard?"

"When I find the right woman. That blue-gray stranger was attractive, might have been interesting had she stuck around. She was chased for a reason."

Kim laughed. "You didn't even get her name!"

"Hey, pillow talk, Kim. That all could come with pillow talk."

Chapter Two

Senior Special Agent Richard Johnson enjoyed his vacation days with simple pleasures. One of the pleasures was watching science fiction and horror movies from his youth. He could enjoy watching a somewhat cheesy older movie without someone expressing their exasperation in his taste of motion picture entertainment with no significant other. He took a sip of his version of a Rusty Nail (Yukon Jack replacing the Dram Bourie with Scotch) and wondered what his married partner Kim Kupar did with her days off. There was a good chance she helped her husband Hank Thomas with his job at the Big Cat House at the

Woodland Park Zoo. Kim's former life involved a stint as a zoology student at the zoo. Richard smiled. It must be nice to have a previous non-law enforcement life in your past. Richard's military and cop work seemed to blur into one long cheap movie. Only, in this film, the protagonist did not seem to get the significant other.

Richard rose from his overstuffed sofa and walked to his kitchen. He had found this older small two-bedroom house out in the boonies a couple of years ago. Located on the southside of Joint Base, Lewis-McChord, living there made his commute into the central Homeland Security Office in downtown Seattle a bit of a trek. However, Richard often worked out of the nearer Tacoma sub-office. Since the formation of the Why Files, the powers that be left Kim and him alone. The bosses liked the high-profile cases they solved, but they also kept them at arm's length due to the 'spookiness' involved.

The house did have a remodeled kitchen and a garage not remodeled into a Mother-In-Law residence as with so many other similar structures. Thus, his Jeep SUV had a home, as did his G-Ride. Richard found a bag of microwave popcorn and refreshed his drink while he waited for it to finish popping. He used some buttery spray and then went back to his television viewing.

"Let me see," Richard said, "*Rodan* or *Them!?* Hmmm. *Rodan*, as I haven't watched it in a while."

He inserted the DVD into the combination television and player, then sat back on the couch and began stuffing his face. Richard reached the point where the prehistoric insects began killing the Japanese miners when he heard an odd humming sound. He stepped up to the television to see if the humming was coming from the DVD player when he noticed the far well seemed to be glowing.

"What the—"

Something morphed through the wall like a hot knife in butter. Automatic reactions took over as the senior special agent grabbed a five-shot snub-nosed revolver he kept near him. Suddenly a bipedal figure took form in front of his eyes as he stepped around behind the sofa.

"Freeze right there!" he yelled out in English, then Spanish, as he calculated his chances of reaching the tactical shotgun in his coat closet by the front door. Then as the shape solidified into something identifiable, his eyes widened.

"You!" he called out as he recognized the attractive, well-built female with bluish skin. Richard and Kim had never been able to put a name or any identity the last time she had appeared—a month prior. Richard swiftly moved towards the shotgun in the closet as he remembered what had followed the woman the last time they met. The lady saw him, her eyes focused and just as she seemed about to speak, she collapsed.

Richard recovered the shotgun, then moved to his visitor. He managed to find a human-type pulse in her wrist and checked her breathing. It seemed in line with human norms, whatever that meant related to a being with bluish skin. Richard picked the woman up and carried her and the shotgun into his bedroom. He had slept on the couch the previous night after falling asleep watching some old outer space epic, so the bed had undisturbed clean sheets. He lay the dark-haired woman on the bed. Then, still lugging around the twelve-gauge, went to the kitchen and fetched a glass of ice water. Richard gently lifted the lady's upper body and held the ice water to her lips. The ice water brought her out of the funk and she eagerly drank the water. Richard laid her back down and refilled the glass in the bathroom sink. The female being finished this glass also and Richard retrieved a third glass of water. The third glass of water the woman sipped at and smiled.

"Well, the smile. Universal facial expressions among us hominids," said Richard with a smile. He then made eating motions and the visitor nodded her head affirmatively.

Richard went to his kitchen, grabbed a loaf of bread, a tub of spreadable butter, a jar of jam and a couple of cheese slices. He returned to the bedroom to see the woman still sipping at the glass of water. Richard sat down in a chair near the bed and used his flick knife to spread butter and jam on the bread. As he did, he handed the stranger the slices of cheese, which she consumed in a flash. Richard saw that her teeth were not filed nor pointed, so he assumed he was in no danger of being eaten.

The strange blueish woman ate three bread, butter, and jam sandwiches in record time as Richard refilled the water glass. The stranger smiled at him after finishing the third sandwich. Richard gestured, 'More?' and the woman shook her head, 'No.' Richard decided this meeting they would get to introductions straight off.

"Richard," he said as he poked his chest.

The woman nodded, then touched her left breast, and

said, "Ariya."

"Well, that's a start." Richard then placed his hands together and laid his cheek on it. The universal sign for 'sleep' worked as Ariya yawned, nodded, 'Yes,' smiled, and laid back on a pillow. She was out like a light.

Richard took a spare bed cover from the pantry closet and spread it over the sleeping Ariya. The senior special agent watched her breathe for a couple of minutes, then went back to the living room. He turned the sound down on the television and finished watching *Rodan*, with an eye and an ear to the bedroom. Richard cleaned up his dishes, then found a shot glass. He poured some Scotch in it and set it next to the water glass as Aila slept. Richard made sure the bedroom window was locked, slid an overstuffed chair next to the open bedroom door. With the shotgun in reach, Richard went to sleep.

Richard woke up early and tiptoed into the bedroom. Ariya was still in a deep sleep. Richard slid back outside the room and went to the kitchen. He took stock of his pantry and refrigerator. Just like many a bachelor, Richard had a lot of microwavable popcorn and snacks. There was also had a single egg and some old ice cream in the freezer.

"I'm going to have to go shopping," he mumbled. How would he do that without leaving the stranger alone? Richard toasted some bread and scrambled the lone egg. He then put the food on a plate and took it to the bedroom.

Ariya was waking up and must have smelled the food. She grinned as he set the food down. He handed a butter knife and a fork to her and the woman inhaled the eggs. She then buttered the toast and ate that. As she finished the plate, she noticed the shot of Scotch. Ariya smiled and threw it back in one gulp. Richard refilled her water glass with ice and fresh water. Ariya began drinking as Richard sat down on a chair next to the bed.

"Well, I'll have to get you some more food, my dear."

Ariya pointed to the plate and said, "Food."

"Yep. I guess you will learn my English faster than I can learn your language. Now, let me show you the plumbing."

Ariya was a quick study on the bathroom devices and Richard gave her the necessary privacy. Then, he showed her the bathtub and turned on the hot water.

"Bath," he said. The woman smiled and touched the warm water with her fingers. She began to strip out of the blue jumpsuit she wore, and Ricard went to get some spare towels. He also found an old t-shirt and sweatpants for Ariya to wear after the bath. The stranger slipped into the warm water with no attempt to hide her nudity, which Richard saw was definitely female. Richard grabbed some dish soap and squirted some under the tap of running water. As the bath turned into a bubble bath, Ariya let out a healthy laugh.

"Yep. We may have different skin colors, but I think we are still of related species."

Ariya flashed a sly smile and motioned Richard to join her in the bath. Now it was Richard's time to laugh.

"Not yet, my dear. While you enjoy your bath, I'll see about getting some more food."

Richard went to his front room and found his cell

phone. It was close to seven AM, so Richard decided he would risk abusing his friendship with Kim. He hit the speed dial on his cellphone and waited. His work partner picked it up on the third ring.

"It must be important for you to be up this early," said Kim.

"Yes, it is. Could I be so bold as to ask you to come over this afternoon, say about one? I have a guest with whom I will need some help. I think you'll find her interesting."

"You haven't got yourself jammed up with some young sweet thing, have you?"

"Kim, you know me better than that."

"Yes, I do. Sorry. But you have piqued my interest. You need Hank for anything?"

"No. It might be better if you came alone."

"Now you really have me wondering. See you at one."

Richard broke the connection and went to the kitchen. He found some tea bags and boiled some water. Searching, the special agent found a few not too old cookies and a partial package of party crackers. Finding a metal serving tray he forgot he had, he put two cups of hot water on the tray, arranged the cookies and crackers, and went back into the bedroom.

Richard knocked on the bathroom door and Ariya said something that must have meant, "Come in." He slowly walked in and displayed the tray of tea and cookies.

Ariya grinned and rose out of the tub with some soap bubbles still attached to her body.

Richard tried to avert his gaze from her curves and

naughty bits as Ariya grabbed a couple of cookies and began munching, standing up in the tub. With the other hand, she took a cup of tea and sipped it, then grinned with cookie crumbs still stuck to her lips.

Richard laughed. "We definitely need to stock up my food stores, young lady."

The special agent started to set the tray down on the sink, and Ariya stepped out of the tub.

"Ah," Richard never got past the 'ah' as the bluish-skinned woman had him wrapped in a tight embrace. She pulled his head down and kissed him long and deep. Richard's hands grasped her firm and shapely buttocks, then caught himself. He tried to untangle himself, but the stranger would have none of that. Ariya wrapped strong legs around his waist and kept kissing him. His male desire took over, and Richard carried the wet woman to the bed.

Richard was unsure about the passage of time but found himself lying next to a sleeping and slightly snoring Ariya. His Earth anatomy had fit perfectly with the alien woman's exquisite body. His mind said that even though she had all the right parts in the right places, her skin color and method of arrival bespoke of an alien from someplace else. Richard slowly slipped out of bed and padded to the kitchen. He dug through the refrigerator and found a can of beer. The federal agent sat at his kitchen table and sipped the beer.

"What have you got yourself into, boyo?"

He glanced at the kitchen clock. Ten AM. He still had some three hours before Kim arrived to compose himself and ensure there was no misunderstanding between him and his visitor. She had come on to him, but few people would believe it, given the weird situation. He finished the beer and walked back to the bedroom. Ariya watched him re-enter the room with a coquettish smile.

"Anybody ever says, Ariya, that you are an energizer bunny rabbit?"

Ariya patted the bed next to her.

"One moment, please."

Richard went to the other bedroom that doubled as a study and returned with some notebook paper, a clipboard, pens and colored pencils. He sat down next to the strange beauty, drew a quick stick figure, and pointed to him.

"Me, Richard."

He then tried to create a crude comic strip to explain who he was and his activities. Ariya caught on quickly and took the paper and writing utensils from him. In a flash with a unique skill, Ariya had drawn a storyboard of her recent life. Richard examined it and pointed to a figure which could only represent the robotic warrior type, which had tried to capture her at their first meeting.

Richard pointed at the figure, and Ariya said, "Skara." The woman frowned as she identified the being. She then pointed to herself and said, "Madiyan."

Richard put his arm around Ariya before he realized what he was doing. *Typical misplaced male protectiveness*, he thought. However, that did not stop him from doing it, gently squeezing her arm and feeling some muscle under the soft female flesh. Ariya kissed him on the cheek, followed by a kiss on the mouth, then their hands were roaming each other's bodies.

A half-hour later and Ariya was in the kitchen finishing off the freezer-burned ice cream as if it were the most delicious meal ever. Richard popped a bag of popcorn in the microwave oven as he pondered the situation. He looked at the gorgeous female in his kitchen who seemed fixated with food and fornication.

"Are you using me, my dear?" he asked.

She smiled in between bites of ice cream. Richard retrieved the pens, pencils, and paper from the earlier communication attempt and sat down at the table. Ariya took the last spoon full of ice cream and sat the empty carton in the kitchen sink. She sat next to Richard and kissed him on the cheek.

"Okay. Work time, not playtime. Got it?"

Ariya smiled as she took the paper from him. In a flash, she was writing in the hieroglyphic-like style Kim and he had first seen in the detention cell. A minute later, Ariya pointed to a symbol, then to Richard with a questioning look on her face.

"I'm Richard, but I think you want to know what I am."

The agent pointed to the symbol and then to him.

"Earthman. I am an Earthman."

Ariya grinned. Then she patted her chest and said, "Ariya…Devon."

Richard grabbed a pencil and another piece of paper.

As fast as he could with his limited artistic ability, he drew a Sol system model. He pointed to the third circle from the sun and then wrote Earth across it.

"Earth," Richard said. He swept his arm around and said, "Earth — here. Devon..." He did the best at creating a questioning facial expression. On another piece of paper, Ariya drew a duplicate solar system, then wrote the symbol for what Richard thought was Devon as she spoke the name aloud.

"Devon. Here—" and Ariya added the plus sign.

"Well, we have one universal symbol. A plus sign for addition."

For the next hour, the two humanoids scribbled and drew various pictures, pointed around the kitchen, and named objects. The language Ariya spoke seemed almost Near Eastern in tone and inflection. Richard had picked up a few words in Iraqi and Afghani in his travels. The words she said just felt like that to Richard. The federal agent soon realized that Ariya was picking up English a helluva lot quicker than Richard was picking up Devonian.

Richard was right about his original assessment that there were connected String Theory Universes with near-duplicate planets.

"I-come-here," Ariya said. "Three times, I-here."

"Why here?" Richard asked.

"I move fast. Here. Skara. They-come also. Soon."

"Why?"

"I am Madiyan."

"Which is?"

The still nude woman (why did he not ask her to put clothes on?) stood up and began to caress her breasts, then ran her hands between her thighs, smiling.

"You are... for sex?"

"Yes. And later, small Madiyans."

Richard took his eyes off her long enough to see it was 12:30.

"Kim, the woman you saw last time would be here." He grabbed his cellphone and scrolled through the photos until he found one of Kim Kupar.

"We work together," Richard said as he displayed the photo.

"Oh! The fighter." Ariya looked at him. "She comes to see me?"

"Yes, to help me. We have to keep you from the Skara."

Again, Ariya flashed her coy smile. "You want me to stay. You want a bath with—"

"No. Yes. I mean, I want you to be safe. But it is not all about rolling around on the bed."

"Will Kim roll around also?"

"Not with us. Kim has Hank."

"Oh. Sad. I, very much like Kim, would want to roll around with her. She would be a good Madiyan."

Richard sighed. Talk about a clash of cultures. "Right now, please put on the sweatsuit bottom I brought for you. Along with the shirt. Here, we wear clothes ninety-nine percent of the time."

"Why?"

"We just do. Now please, for me?" Ariya stepped forward and put a lip lock on Richard that he would not forget. The alien shoved him back with a giggle and danced to the bedroom.

Houston, we have a problem, Richard thought as he tried to calm himself.

K im showed up right on time.
  "So, what is so—*you!*" Kim exclaimed as she saw Ariya step from the bedroom with a Cheshire cat smile.

"Hello, Kim," Ariya said. "You roll around with Hank, yes?"

"Kim, meet Ariya."

The bluish-skinned alien stepped up and hugged the surprised female agent. "You are strong, Kim. Richard, are you sure Kim not—"

"Please do not start that again. Now, Kim. I desperately need to go out and get a bunch of food. Ariya has an extremely high metabolism."

Kim untangled herself from Ariya and gave her a once-over. "How long has she been here?"

"Last night. She slept like a log, then a bath this morning."

"We rolled around also," said Arya with a mischievous grin.

"Now, Kim, it's not like—"

"Take a breath, partner. I am the last person to judge bed mates after having one trying to kill me."

"I won't be gone long."

"Take your time. Ariya and I will get acquainted. I have a lot of questions to ask her."

"You can make some of that tea you gave me, Kim."

"Okay." Kim stepped over and picked up the shotgun. "Just in case Ariya has another visitor."

Richard went to the nearest Big Box Store and filled up a cart, grabbing some feminine-looking sweats and some feminine hygiene products in addition to all types of food. He loaded a couple of bottles of wine, some soda pop, and some juices; also stocked up on frozen pizza, hamburger meat, chicken, canned tuna, bread, and soft tortillas in the cart. Richard topped it off with some snack cakes, potato chips, popcorn, and a couple of cartons of ice cream.

Richard found Kim sitting at the dining table with a pizza's remains as she used her laptop.

"Ariya is sleeping," said Kim. "I ordered a meat lover's pizza when you left, and the food got her talking. She has picked up English super-fast with some help from my laptop."

"So, what did you find out?" Richard asked as he put the food away.

"Well, first, 'Madiyan' seems to be from Old Persian and means 'mare' or 'broodmare.' That word seems to match our new friend's heightened sexuality. Someone raised Ariya to desire sex of all types, and I daresay will perform the street vernacular of popping babies out like hotcakes."

"You two must have had a fascinating conversation."

"Yes, Richard. She also asked me if I wanted to have sex with her, which I politely refused. Sexual congress seems to be her quick way of bonding with people. Some sexual abuse victims have that reaction, thinking people will only like them if they perform sexually. However, Ariya seems more like a woman bred to be a succubus."

"A succubus?"

"Sex used as power and control. I would not be surprised to find that Ariya's owners or handlers used her to control others and then eventually produce the next generation of succubi."

"But Ariya had the free will to escape."

"Which brings us to the word 'Skara,' which seems to be Old Persian for 'hunter.' Her previous handlers wanted her back."

"Well, her food intake seems indicative she has been on the run for a while with limited resources."

"Add the metabolism of an energizer bunny and she has an eat, activity, sex, sleep, cycle."

The two agents were quiet as Richard finished putting the food away. Then, Richard asked, "What's next?"

"You know we have to turn her in."

"Why? I have some leave coming. I could help Ariya become acclimated; eventually, she is smart enough to find a job, a career..."

"Richard, you are thinking with your small head rather than the large one on your shoulders. She is technically an illegal alien; arresting them is part of our job."

Richard sat across from his partner and sighed. "Yes. Shit. It's not Ariya's fault she is trying to escape from sexual bondage."

"If she came from a known country in our world, we could treat her as a sex trafficking victim. But when someone realizes she comes from an actual other universe... well, then Men in Black will show up."

Ariya stepped from the bedroom, and Richard rose to meet her.

"Hey. I bought something for you to wear plus lots of eats."

"You are talking about what to do with me," Ariya said.

"Too smart for us," said Richard. "We have to figure out what to do. It is part of our job."

Ariya sat down at the table as Richard handed her the female workout gear. The blue-skinned woman grinned. "This will fit better," she said.

"You learned our language quickly," said Richard.

"It is an... *ability* I think the word is. I have some parts of my body; additions added to help me dealing with others."

"So, you can move again," said Kim.

"Yes. Let me show you."

Ariya opened up her mouth and removed a dental bridge from the back of her mouth.

"Look at the circuits. They connect with others in my bones. I can find weak spots between universes. At the right moment, I can move through."

"Why did your masters give you this ability if you can use it to flee?" Asked Kim.

"Because the Skara exists. They rarely fail."

"But they have in your case," said Richard.

"Because you killed one. The one you killed and kept the body—it is the first in decades of your time."

"They still hunt for you," stated Kim.

"Yes. I moved many times. I was lucky to find Richard's home."

Richard looked at Kim and then spoke. "They will dissect her like an insect if we turn her in. Just like they would dissect Sir Khan if they catch him."

"Trying to use him as an argument is not fair, Richard. My feelings connected with him have nothing to do with Ariya."

"Sir Khan?" asked Ariya.

"A creature, who like you, was created and abused for selfish reasons," replied Kim.

The three humanoids lapsed into silence. Kim finally spoke. "Ariya, can you tell if a location has no weak spots which allow travel between the string universes?"

"Yes, although the skin of the universes shifts in their connections."

"Why were you created then?"

Ariya paused, then answered, "We are used to—sneak in and steal items from other places. My kind seduces the powerful, makes them weak and easy to rob."

"You do this your entire life?" Richard asked.

"Until I age to a point and then I am bred. My added memory core tells me I can have two or more children every time I am impregnated and allowed to give birth."

"If one of you becomes pregnant when they are not supposed to when they have not been retired, what happens?"

"The life is killed in the womb."

Richard could tell when the darker-skinned Kim flushed with anger. "Forced abortions. Sick alien bastards." Kim fixed her partner agent with a stare, which told Richard she had made a difficult decision.

"Ariya, Richard, and I are going to have to work keeping you safe. If I can ask you to watch some television in the bedroom which will help you learn more about our Earth—"

"Of course, my new friend. If I can have a carton of that food, you call ice cream."

A day later, Ariya met Mike Johnson, Richard's father, at his acreage in Port Orchard.

"I know I am asking a lot."

"You're my son, Richard. It's not a lot."

"This is illegal—"

"Well, since Ariya did not sneak across the border, I say she is not an illegal alien. I propose she is a refugee dumped here. Some modern make-up will help with her unusual skin color when she is in public. Besides, kids these days have all kinds of tattoos."

"Kim and I are setting up the equivalent of a tiger pit for the assholes looking for her. They should pop up at my place first."

"Our dogs are useful early warning and Mom and I have plenty of firepower. Ariya seems to be getting along just fine with the dogs."

"They are a good judge of character, Dad."

Richard walked over to where four dogs mobbed Ariya with canine affection. Richard finally managed to separate her from the dogs and walked her to the house.

"My mom and dad will look after you. All they ask is you help around this place with the livestock and upkeep."

Ariya hugged him tightly. "You will visit? Often? I know Kim thinks I am just a succubus, but I feel—different around you."

Richard kissed her. "Let's see if we can make this work. Hopefully, some of the hormone and blood workup at the zoo lab done on the sly can help you resist sex with every young male around. Mom will not like it if you start looking funny at my dad."

"I do have some control, Richard. Please trust me."

"I understand. Now, kiss me goodbye so Kim and I can set up the tiger pit."

It took a week with Kim, Richard, and Hank, Kim's husband, camped out at Richard's home for the trap to spring. The shimmering on the living room wall happened at noon one day. Two Skaras stepped through and froze as the holographic display kicked into action. Richard had to call in some favors from some tech guys he knew to set up the equipment. As the hunters tried to figure out what was real and what was not, large game crossbows twanged and sent heavy-duty bolts into the heads of both creatures.

Richard then stepped up and emptied subsonic rounds from a silenced Glock nine-millimeter into the two skulls. Ten bullets each finished the job the crossbow bolts began.

As smokes and sparks emanated from the robotic creatures, Hank stepped up and swung a double-bladed ax, severing the heads from the bodies.

"Your trap worked, Kim," said Richard.

"Duplicating the frequencies and vibrations from Ariya's bridgework worked as a live goat did to rogue tigers in India. Now, we just need to figure how to get these to the Men in Black without them looking for Ariya."

"Well, your friendly Big Cat zookeeper will act as a believable witness that they chased Ariya through your home," said Hank. "I own the crossbows, so the story is still I was showing them to you for a hunting trip."

"The fewer gunshots, the better. The silencer just reduces police response until we can contact the Men in Black, who know us too well already."

"Let's get the holographic equipment out of here. Then, we make phone calls," said Richard. He looked at his two friends. "I know you are both taking a big chance—"

"Sometimes, Pard, you take action because it is right, not because it is legal," Kim said with a wide grin.

"Agent T-Rex Moyer told you that, right?" asked Richard.

"Yes, he did. But I learned something else on my own."

"What's that?"

Kim looked at her husband as she spoke. "Finding and sacrificing for true love has morality and correctness all its own. I hope it works for Ariya and you."

"Hell, with friends like you to help me out, how can it fail?"

A giant sabretooth cat sensed a disturbance in the universe. He sniffed the air, hoping to catch a remembered scent of a favorite human. There was nothing in the Olympic National Forest that seemed out of place, but still, Sir Khan sensed... something. When his pride was secure, Sir Khan would take a trek further south as something was different. The human-made feline searched for and found love. Maybe he sensed another creature had done the same.

Sir Khan would soon find out.

Chapter Three

Richard Johnson was on the second day of a snot-slinging, gutter-hugging binge. He called in sick again this morning to his Homeland Security Investigations office in downtown Seattle. Any desire to go to the job he usually much enjoyed was lacking. The lack of desire started on Sunday, and now it was Tuesday. Richard staggered to his refrigerator to fetch some more ice to add to his watery and cheap Scotch whiskey. He somehow kept from spilling the ice tray contents all over the kitchen floor of his house.

Richard stared at his glass as he added several ounces of the cheap alcohol. "Huh. The bottle is almost gone," the senior special agent mumbled. "Booze is gone, just like Ariya."

Richard stumbled back to his sofa with the glass and ice cube tray, added some ice to his booze and then plopped down. He stared at his widescreen television that played some cheap science-fiction epic. Without his blue-skinned Ariya, the most enjoyable activity of his past was dull. Richard took a large drink from his glass just as someone pounded on his front door.

"Go away," the man yelled. "I don't want any."

Richard heard the sound of a key inserted into the front door lock. He tried to stand and stumble to the entrance, lost his balance and fell. A figure suddenly stood over him and Richard attempted to focus his eyes.

"You're drunk," Kim Kupar, his investigation partner, said as she looked down at him with a frown. "And somehow, you did not spill that drink in your hand."

"Good," he slurred. "I am almost out and can't drive."

Richard sipped at his drink while propped up on one arm. Then Kim expertly snatched the glass from his hand.

"Hey!"

"You have had enough, Richard. Come on, get up. You cannot cry in your beer for the next year."

"It's Scotch, not beer. I have a six-pack of Rainier in my fridge. You want one?"

Kim sighed. To see her partner in this state both frustrated and saddened her. Kim had seen him handle some dangerous situations with hardly breaking a sweat. Now....

"Come on. Get up and I'll make you some breakfast—actually, now lunch."

"I'm not hungry, Kim. You could get me some

more Scotch."

Kim sighed in exasperation. She then bent over and grabbed Richard's nose in a painful grip. With a twist. Kim soon had Richard rising to stand while trying not to spill his drink.

"Ouch. Let go!"

"Not until you walk with me to the kitchen for some food, then the bathroom for a shower. "

"You damn martial arts bully. Come on, let go."

Kim walked Richard and made him sit at the kitchen table. Richard rubbed his bruised nose as he cursed under his breath.

"Why'd you come over here?" asked Richard.

"Your dad called me and told me Ariya had disappeared, leaving a note behind."

Richard's face assumed the look of a sad puppy. "She said she had to get back to her kind. Her skin color... she never thought she would fit in."

"The makeup we developed; it didn't work?"

"Yes, it did, but not in her eyes. She said people still looked at her funny."

Richard finished his drink in a couple of gulps.

"Alright, Richard. That is enough booze. Now sit while I cook you something."

A half-hour later and Richard was chowing down on a cheese and bologna omelet. Kim added a splash of all the spices in his cupboard. She also provided a bunch of toast and a crumbled-up stale donut fried in the leftover cooking pan grease.

"Well, I know another reason why Hank keeps you around. You're a good cook, Kim."

"Both sides of my family tree taught me how to make something tasty and filling with leftovers. Do you feel a bit better?"

"My stomach, yes. My heart, no."

Kim made them both cups of the Indian tea she gave Richard, but he rarely used them. Kim sat down across from her investigative partner and waited for him to speak. After a couple of sips, Richard talked.

"I know I'm acting like a heartsick puppy. I just have never felt like this before."

"Richard, I felt like that after John Wang showed his true colors."

"Well, he was an asshole and is now taking a dirt nap. Ariya was never an asshole. And I love her more than anyone I have ever met."

Kim paused for a moment as she tried to decide just the correct words to use. "Richard, she was not evil, nor the asshole you mention. But someone bred her to be their equivalent of a combined broodmare and temptress. Her kind seduces those in power, as well as steal valuables as they flit between universes. When you have been bred and raised for those functions, it is hard to change."

"Damnit, I know! But... but we worked on it—"

"Yet she still felt a need to leave, maybe because she loves you and doesn't want you hurt or even killed by the Skara hunters."

Richard bolted upright, knocking over his chair. "I

could protect her. I proved that—"

"And it seems she left to protect you. Did you consider that?"

Richard stood and fumed. "It's not fair. I find the love of my life, and she disappears into another dimension. If I could follow her—"

"You would not only give up a career you love, but you would also probably be in some dungeon or dead. Despite the alien technology, the people in her universe seem to have a medieval type of society."

Richard fell silent, then plopped back into his chair. "I need a drink," said the agent.

"No," replied Kim. "You need to sober up. I have an overnight bag in my car. I'll stay here and watch old sci-fi movies with you, give you tomorrow to recover also. I'll tell the bosses you have a nasty case of food poisoning."

Richard looked at Kim. "Why are you doing this? Sticking your neck out like this? You have Hank waiting at home."

Kim smiled as she answered. "Because you hard-headed old border rat you, you're my partner. My 'Pard' as T-Rex Moyer told me. And Pards have each other's backs."

Richard looked at Kim for a few moments before he spoke. "I owe you and do not deserve you as a friend."

"Well, you're stuck with me. Now, take a shower, put some clean clothes on and we'll restock your larder. Eggs and bologna are not exactly my choice of food."

Later that evening, Kim made up the hide-a-bed sofa in the living room for her sleeping spot. Sleeping next to her investigative partner in his was just a bit too close. And she wanted to make sure she could keep Richard from sneaking out for some alcohol to self-medicate.

"You sure you want to sleep here for the next couple of nights?" asked Richard.

"Yes. Then on Thursday, we can go to the office together, and you can tell them just how sick you were."

"Okay. Well, good night Kim, AKA Raptor."

"Goodnight, John Boy."

"That is not my handle."

"Okay, Elvis, with your sideburns."

"That's better."

At some 3:00 AM, an all too familiar shimmering woke Kim up. She saw the dining room wall partially dissolve, and Ariya stepped through into this universe. Kim swore under her breath and rose to meet her.

"What are you doing back here?"

"Where is Richard? I must—"

Two Skara machine men hunters took that moment to step through a portal on the opposite living room wall. Ariya screamed as Kim tried to grab her pistol.

"What the hell—" called out Richard from his bedroom.

An immense shape crashed through the sliding glass back door and slammed into the Skara. Large clawed paws smashed the mechanical creatures around before the predator used near twelve-inch fangs to crush the humanoid shaped skulls. Then all was quiet. Richard stood at his bedroom door with his mouth agape, unable to speak. Kim lunged, grabbed Ariya, and shoved her through the closing portal from whence she came.

Richard cried out and dashed towards the exit spot of Ariya, and Kim tackled him to the floor. There was a familiar popping sound as the doorway to another universe snapped shut. Richard broke free from Kim's grasp and leaped to his feet.

"Why in the fuck did you do that? Why did you push Ariya back to her universe?"

"Because she does't belong here, Richard. She will always be coming and going and dragging those hunter things with her. Someday, they will kill us or someone else."

"But I love her!"

"And just like John Wang and me, that love will kill you."

Richard stared at Kim, then his shoulders drooped. "Why is this love shit so hard?" he asked.

"The human condition, my friend."

Then both humans noticed the many hundreds of pound cat in the room.

"Ah, what is Sir Khan doing here?" asked Richard in a low voice.

"I had to keep him secret. He came to your dad's place in Kitsap County. I think he can sense people like Ariya or things that don't belong in this world."

The oversized human-made sabretooth cat sidled up to Kim, shoved her with his massive head. Kim began to scratch his ears.

"So, is he friendly to me?"

"Yes. Sir Khan knows you are my friend. But just like Ariya, we have to keep this quiet. Or, the Men in Black will dissect him in some laboratory. This cat is way above the norm in intelligence. They will want to see what makes him tick and then—a new weapon."

Richard looked at Sir Khan, then at the destroyed French sliding door. "Great entrance. Now, we have to fix a door and hide an oversize feline, not to mention the Skara. How do we explain the bodies?"

"We dump them in the forest, away from everybody, in case more come looking."

"Okay, Kim. But let's make a deal. This incident is the last mystery we hide. The more lies, the deeper the crap gets."

"Agreed. I'll squeeze Sir Khan back into my van and run him to the Peninsula. But only after we get rid of the Skara."

"You mean, Sir Khan hides here? I guess the garage will temporarily serve as a hideaway."

"It is only for a few hours."

"Okay. Let's get cracking."

Hours later, Kim and Richard collapsed on the now-folded up couch bed.

"Here, Richard. Have a beer with the pizza."

"Not afraid I'll go on a binge?"

"Nope. I think you are past that."

As the two friends ate pizza and drank beer, they

talked about love lost and found. Finally, Richard belched.

"Well, one thing is sure, Kim."

"What is that, my friend and comrade?"

"Just like in that song, love hurts."

"It can, Richard. It surely can."

Chapter Four

Kim Kupar handed Richard Johnson his extra-large cup of coffee.

"Extra Irish Cream-flavored creamer as you like it," Kim said with a smile.

"I wish this surveillance van had a toilet in here," Richard stated.

"Why? You want me to watch you urinate?"

"No. I don't want to have to sneak out to the local Mcfrackers when my bladder is full and risk one of those assholes in that fleabag motel see me."

"The motel is two blocks away, Richard. The cameras whose feed we are watching are well hidden in that beater of a car you found. The chances of being seen are slight."

"Yeah, but not zero. This Senior Special Agent does not want to explain how I blew this surveillance on a child trafficking case."

"I guess I am lucky I am still just a Special Agent. You, as the senior agent, get to face the heat."

The agents and others had been sitting on the seedy motel north of Seattle for over a week. An informant had come forward with detailed information about the illegal operation. A former motel maid, the Mexican national illegally in the United States, risked deportation to bring Homeland Security Investigations cellphone photos of scared children of various ethnicities jammed together in a couple of rooms. There were clearly no parents or relatives around.

"If I had my druthers, I would summarily execute the scum-sucking snakeheads," growled Richard.

"Well, partner, you know we can't do that."

"I know. But I can dream, can't I?"

"Let me contact Brenna; see if she has noticed anything."

Brenna Freiberg from U.S. Fish and Wildlife was another permanent member of the Why Files Investigation. Brenna had been with the Why Files from the very beginning, her tall blonde Nordic persona providing a contrast to Kim's darker Argentine and Punjabi ancestry.

Brenna answered her cellphone with, "Anything new?"

"No. You and Dennis Spain doing okay?"

Brenna laughed. "This cold weather fits my Norse genes just fine. I'm trying to keep my African American partner here well supplied with hot coffee."

"This is not Texas weather," they overheard Dennis say. The HSI Agent was newly assigned to the group after working with Kim on some previous cases, including the Jade Eyes investigation. An attempted NFL linebacker who just missed the cut to pro, his physicality and Lotario good looks added an extra dimension to the inquiry.

"You can say that again," said Richard over the

speakerphone. "Border Rats miss the dry heat."

"Why'd you come here?" Dennis asked.

"Family. I was born here in the Northwest. But my body prefers the Southwest."

The four agents were not alone in the surveillance. A marked King County Sheriffs' two-person car and a four-person Border Patrol tactical response team had parked at different compass points a half-mile away.

"So please explain again why we can't get a search warrant and hit the motel now, Mr. Senior Case Agent."

"We have to refresh the informant's information. She waited some three days out of fear to bring us the cell phone photos. A judge will ask, 'are those kids still there' and if we say, 'as of three days ago,' he or she will smile and look at the Assistant U.S. Attorney assigned to this case with a raised eyebrow. The AUSA will know the eyebrow means the information is not current enough and then huff and puff for us wasting time. Thus, I cross that bridge before there is a question."

Kim smiled. "Which is why you are a Senior Special Agent."

"Nah. I just stuck around long enough that management had to promote me to the level of my incompetence—the Peter Principle."

The team sat quietly for an hour. Richard had lost count of the hours he had spent on such operations. Sit and wait, sit and wait. People in the civilian world had no idea what unlike Hollywood epics actual law enforcement was like, how boring it was usually. That, and how they consumed so much lukewarm coffee. Richard sipped at his and was about to ask Kim if she wanted to make a coffee run when he heard the dreaded "Oh, shit."

"What's up?"

"There is an odd glow—"

Richard looked at the surveillance screen. Then he began to curse. "Oh. No. Not again. Not here. I thought we were done with that, with Ariya."

"Wait. Let me zoom in, Richard."

The video screen quickly displayed a close-up shot of a bluish glow from a room on the second floor, directly above the manager's office.

"It could be anything—a decorative light, a television screen—"

"Bullshit. I've seen that way too many times."

"But why here, now?"

"We'll have to ask her—or them." Richard got on the government radio. "Brenna, move in. We have something… strange. Take a look."

Moments later, the Fish and Wildlife Agent responded. "We have a large van moving into the front of the manager's office; stand by."

Kim began adjusting the zoom on the prepositioned cameras just as the van quickly pulled up to the manager's office main door. Someone slammed open the sliding side door of the vehicle and shoved a small figure out. Another and another followed the first, as someone opened the manager's office door from inside. All the human shapes had hoods over their heads, causing several to stumble and fall against the office wall.

"Those are kid-sized bodies," said Kim.

"We go in. Fuck the search warrant, exigent circumstances," growled Richard as he grabbed his MP-5 submachine gun.

"You sure, partner?" asked Kim.

"I'll risk losing a case rather than have those kids transported to God knows where for God knows what."

Richard yelled a 'Go Code' over the radio as he jumped into the surveillance van's driver seat and gunned the engine. The vehicle tires squealed as he did a U-turn and sped down the two blocks to the motel. Brenna and Dennis arrived just as Richard and Kim did.

Someone inside the human transport vehicle panicked and fired a shot at Kim and Richard, cracking the passenger side front windshield and narrowly missing Kim. The female agent leapt from the van and returned fire with her assault rifle. Two well-aimed shots splattered the brains of the shooter around the cab of the transport van. The driver accelerated into the motel parking area. Two small bodies were thrown to the ground as they fell from the open side door while Richard bellowed in anger.

"Police! Federal agents! *Freeze!*"

The U.S. Border Patrol Tactical Team SUV screeched to a halt as the agents leapt from the vehicle. Seconds later, the Sheriffs showed up. The motel was of aged design with just one way in and out, no back door for escape. The miscreants' van U-turned at the back of the parking lot and smashed into the only other parked car. Knocking the smaller vehicle out of the way, the driver accelerated towards the law enforcement vehicles.

Richard took a chance to miss any other kidnapped children in the fleeing vehicle and fired a short burst of his MP-5 at the driver's side. The agent's aim was dead on; the driver jerked the wheel as his foot slipped off the accelerator, and he died. The van continued and hit the rear of the blocking surveillance van and halted.

Kim was in the manager's office as Brenna and Dennis caught up to her. Children's and young people's voices screamed in fear in several languages as Kim dashed past the hooded figures and pursued a masked shape. Kim ran up the stairs to the second floor and the source of the bluish light. She caught up with the supposed motel manager just as he stepped towards the far wall of the upstairs living space. The wall had dissolved into an all too well-known depression serving as Alice in Wonderland's rabbit hole. The female Special Agent tripped the fleeing person by jamming her rifle between the running legs. The head and shoulders of a humanoid appeared, its hands and arms reaching for the sprawled figure. Kim threw herself at the reaching person and disappeared through the portal. Brenna, right behind, screamed and leapt after Kim.

The tactical team secured the criminal's van, ensured there were no occupants other than the two dead men. The Sheriff's deputies kept the dozen hooded children and teenagers in the motel lobby and office area and called for backup as Dennis and Richard scrambled up the stairs to the manager's living space. They arrived in time to see large

Brenna dragging Kim and another figure back through the portal, seconds before it closed with a 'popping' noise. Dennis grabbed the fallen supposed manager and yanked the mask off. He yelped when he saw the face entirely covered with hair like a Hollywood werewolf. Richard covered the wolfman and the figure Kim and Brenna had in their grip. He swore when they removed the face covering of that individual. A dark blue feminine individual stared at him. It was not Ariya, although it could have been a cousin.

"I hate being right sometimes," said Richard.

Assistant Special Agent in Charge Tim Weiss showed up soon after other backup law enforcement appeared. He looked at Richard and Kim and smiled as he shook his head. "You just had to find another case to draw the Men in Black, didn't you?"

"Hey, the Why Files don't ask for them, boss. They just—happen."

"Well, Richard, they will be here soon. You have aliens from some other world or universe, plus young kidnapped kids about to be taken somewhere not of this world. Somehow, we have a bunch of people to swear to secrecy as we try to return those twelve minors to their families."

"At least we can return them, sir," said Kim. "A few more minutes and they would be out of our reach."

"Which is why if this went to trial, no one would question your assault on these assholes. Even though a surveillance van is not supposed to be a roadblock."

"The two dead men. From here?"

"Yes. Earth human, Kim. Our Chewbacca-looking one and Blueskin will have some explaining to do to the Men in Black. Now, get to the office and start doing the preliminary paperwork. Child Protective Services will help us locate the families."

Kim walked over to Brenna, feeding the rescued kids some fast food and joking with them. For a large Shieldmaiden, Brenna had a way with children.

"Hey, Brenna, have a minute?"

"Sure. Be right back with some more eats, young ones."

There were some smiles and comments in several languages as Brenna walked with Kim. In the shadows, Kim hugged the tall blonde woman. "I owe you my life. Why you took such a chance diving through that wormhole—"

"You are a friend and a teammate. Of course, I dove in after you, Kim. You would do the same for me."

"But I'm not sure I could drag your tall frame back as you did me. Remember that before you go diving through shimmering holes into another universe!"

"Well, it worked out. I now know more about some of the events you and Richard have spoken about in your reports. Fire-breathing dragons are not our biggest worry. We now have interdimensional and maybe interplanetary kidnappers."

Kim sighed. "Yes. We have a whole new group of threats to look for as we do our investigations. But, with people like you watching my back, we will succeed."

Brenna gave Kim a parting hug and walked back to the

kids. They would need reassurance for quite some time that this would not happen to them again.

"I swear to all that is holy; I will *not* allow this to happen again," Kim whispered. Then she walked back towards Richard. It would be a late night of writing reports and securing evidence. There was no rest for the just or the wicked.

There was a shimmering in the Olympic National Forest's mountainous region, and then a popping sound as a duplicate portal to the one at the motel office appeared. Through the doorway stepped two blue-faced male humanoids, followed by a figure known to the Why Files as a Skara Hunter. The two males conferred in their parent language as they surveyed the location for a new portal. It was located at the end of a seldom-used dirt roadway once cut by the U.S. Forest Service. The two males and the Skara humanoid were too involved in checking the new, more remote transfer location that they did not notice the hunting creatures who padded upon their site.

The largest one sprang into action as soon as he realized there was a Skara in *his* forest. Sir Khan's mate and their young leapt onto the three figures. Sir Khan decapitated the Skara Hunter with a twist of his sabretooth jaws as the two Blue Skins screamed until the cougar sabretooth cat hybrids ripped out their throats. The three cubs sniffed at the odd meat, then stepped away in disgust, as did their mother. Sir Khan walked up to his mate and his offspring, affectionally bumping into each one. Then he growled at the still-open portal. A third Blue Skin began to step through and Sir Khan slammed it back to its world with a smashing top clawed paw. The doorway popped shut.

The Feline King of the Forest stared at the dead figures, then at the area of the now-closed portal. He had dealt with this problem before when he helped the upright two-legged monkey known as the Tiger Lady. His superior intellect told Sir Khan he would have to deal with these—things—again. Their presence would also bring the Tiger Lady back. That was a good thing. Sir Khan had a unique connection with the human, which he enjoyed.

Until then, Sir Khan marked his territory with his urine. Then he let the rest of the forest know who ruled here. A loud and unique big cat roar reverberated through the woods.

This forest is *mine*, roared Sir Khan. Woe to those who trespass.

Chapter Five

David Mooney sat in the former U.S. Postal Service Jeep outside the run-down apartments in Port Angeles. The forty-year-old man with a bit of a beer gut lost count of the number of nights he had spent watching the comings and goings from this location. He didn't care. The recent raid on a motel in Seattle and the recovery of many young kids involved in human trafficking for God knew what purposes justified his suspicions, at least in his mind.

David slurped his coffee and then used his battered binoculars to check the room windows he could see. The building had a total of twelve one-bedroom and studio apartments, all facing out on the street. In reality, the street was the upper end of Mount Pleasant Road as it ran in a westerly direction out of the town proper. The apartments' reputation existed as a place for transients, illegal aliens, dopers, prostitutes and parolees. The management rented supposedly by the month but often by the week, which should have classified it as a hotel. However, no one in the town/ county government took the time to enforce those regulations. The owners paid the taxes on time, never complained to the town council, so people in power ignored the infractions.

David tried to alert the local authorities about what he observed even before the articles about the raid in Seattle by Homeland Security Agents hit the remaining newspapers and the Internet. However, they blew him off. David had a problem. He had proposed so many conspiracy theories over the previous decade that people wrote him off as the Aluminum Foil Hat Brigade leader.

David Mooney was always seen as odd while growing up. His mother said he marched to the beat of a different drummer. His father said there was no drummer; David just heard voices in his head. His younger brother Donald and his two older sisters, Fay and Alice, always seemed embarrassed by his oddness. David, from an early age, embraced the strange and bizarre and rambled about it. He seemed brilliant in math and the sciences, had what it seemed was a photographic memory, so school work was easy. However, his weirdness led him to be shunned by many.

David's father convinced him to sign up for the U.S. Air Force to receive technical training, funds for college and get him away from the house. He made it through basic training because of his ability to copy what the instructors did and said precisely while other trainees screwed up. Thus, David dodged the wrath of the drill instructors and higher ranks. They did recognize him as an 'egghead' and pushed him to engineer and science relater career fields. But leadership skills? David had none.

David made it through four years of the military and then it was politely suggested he go to college rather than risk a rather embarrassing psychological examination and profile. David showed signs of fixations with conspiracies and the weird to the point the word 'schizophrenic' appeared in conversations about him. David was aware enough to realize he did not fit in the military and took the advice. David soon had a degree in computer science and advanced mathematics, then a job with a big tech firm. His early success attracted a woman or two and he married, had children, and a lovely home.

Then David began claiming he saw aliens and portals to other universes. The man claimed 'blue people' were watching him and talking to him on his computer. David tried to alert the authorities in D.C. about these Aliens so many times that his employer fired him, his wife left him, he lost his home. He moved in with his brother Donald, the lawyer, for a short time until they located a suitable apartment.

"David, you have to stop this crap," Donald told him. "You are brilliant, and I love you as a brother, but you cannot keep claiming you saw all these aliens and talk about abductions. You have to get a life."

David almost said, "But this is my life, my reality." However, by now, he knew if he said that, he would be in Western State Psychiatric Hospital as a long-term patient. Donald obtained a job for him with a bail bondsman and private investigation outfit as their intelligence analyst. David was like a dog with a bone when given someone or something to find. This job put him in contact with law enforcement.

Donald had to warn him against his ramblings when people reported allegations of abductions, etc.

"They like the information you provide, the way you can track people down. Do not push your luck."

So, David shut up what he saw around the apartment, not far from where he lived. Then he saw the raid report and the picture of the man arrested with alleged congenital hypertrichosis. People did not know how rare that condition was and that David had seen another such subject at the apartments. He now knew he was right.

David did have a network of people who believed much as he did. The one who provided the most support was Doc Anderson. David was unsure as to what type of doctorate Doc had achieved. But Doc seemed to be able to obtain information and equipment David could not. In a locked trunk in the back of David's former government jeep was an 1800s double-barreled shotgun Doc got from some estate sale with two black powder buckshot shells. Off the record, David could ditch it after use. David's reputation concerning his possible mental problems made his buying weapons difficult.

David's cellphone range. He looked at caller I.D and saw it was his employer, Jeff Samples.

"You rang, Jeff?"

"You going to be in the office tomorrow? And I mean not sleeping at your desk."

The man was old enough to be David's father and treated him like the Prodigal Son.

"Yes, Boss. I will be there and not fall asleep at my desk."

"Okay. We have a rush trace and track job. If we get it done in record time, we get a bonus."

"Okay, see you there."

David watched the apartment for a few more minutes. He thought he saw a flash of bluish light from a curtained window but had to admit his tired eyes may be playing tricks. He yawned, cursed, and drove home.

Ten minutes after he left, an exotic blue light bathed the apartment manager's office in its unique luminance.

David was too busy for a couple of days to work on his 'private case.' He did his magic and helped Jeff complete the track and trace in record time. The employer threw a stack of twenty-dollar bills on his desk.

"Finding a rich man's daughter pays well, David. Take a couple of days off and have some fun, not chase aliens."

David nodded and jammed the bills into his pocket. He started to shut down his computer when an African American couple walked into the office. Their faces exhibited the combined fear, embarrassment and confused look David saw on many new AAA Investigations customers.

"May I help you?" David asked.

"I hope," said the woman. The couple looked to be about forty years of age or older. "We are looking for our daughter, Portia."

"She ran off," interrupted the man. "She's pregnant."

At the comment, the woman began to cry.

David got them to sit down with cups of coffee. John and Talia Strong were from Tacoma, Washington. His boss Jeff was on the phone in his office, so David handled the couple. Portia, the daughter, left them a note she was pregnant and was going with some unknown man to Port Angeles. To say the news and action blindsided the parents was an understatement.

"Portia dated and studied at the Tacoma University of Washington campus but had no steady boyfriend," said Talia, her mother. "And if she were pregnant, she knew we would support her if she wished to keep her baby. We had 'the talk' when she first began having her period."

David looked at John. "Would you agree?"

"If you're saying I'd chase her off, hell no! She is my daughter."

"Any idea where she may be in the Port Angeles area? And mention of Canada?"

"Just this partial scribble on the note she left," answered John. "These four numbers look like part of a street address, but no connected name. Or maybe it's part of a telephone number."

David looked at the four numbers and instantly

recognized them.

"Here. Please sign this contract," David said as he pushed some forms at the couple. "I think I can help you. Come back tomorrow afternoon, and we'll review some initial information. I need to check something out."

"Whatever you can do. We checked around, and some private investigators suggest we contact you up here in Port Angeles," added the mother.

"Glad they liked our work. Okay. See you tomorrow."

Jeff Samples stepped out from his office as the Strongs left. "New clients?" asked his boss.

"Yes. They'll be back tomorrow—Runaway adult daughter, so no law enforcement interest."

"Huh. Well, parents like them keep us in business."

Jeff went back into his office as David looked at the numbers the parents provided. They were of 'his' case subject, the run-down apartments. David did not let on to the Strongs of his knowledge.

If Portia went there, she might be gone forever.

David set up on the apartments on a side road armed with an office camera with night lenses and a photo of Portia the parents provided. She had the good looks of a model. He knew the chances of seeing her were remote, but stranger things had happened. The raid in the Seattle area proved that even if the authorities covered it up.

It was the Witching Hour. David stopped by Doc's laboratory—apartment, in actuality—earlier, and he gave David a small portable radio to call him direct for backup.

David humored him but had no plans to get the older man. If things went sour, he'd call the cops and his boss, not Doc. Now, David sat in his small Jeep with the goodtime radio just loud enough to hear Coast to Coast AM late-night broadcast. The show that night was a review of some Alien Abduction cases. David chuckled. If they only knew the real story.

David sipped his coffee and had a caffeinated soft drink as a backup to keep him awake. He munched on some popcorn and waited.

12:30 AM and a blue glow emanated from the manager's office/apartment. David began filming with the company camera. For once, he could justify its use and not be yelled at for using it on a wild goose chase. David thought all he would see would be the glow he had seen many times below. But having blue lights was not against the law.

Having a young Black woman run screaming from an apartment may point to illegal activities. David cursed, spilled his coffee, and yelled over the radio to Doc to call the police. He stumbled from his vehicle and ran towards the woman.

"Portia!" David yelled, and his guess on identity was correct as the woman responded to his yell and made a beeline towards him.

"My baby! My baby!" Portia screamed as she collapsed into David's arms. He looked towards the apartments and froze. Running from the manager's office area was two large baboons. Or at least things that resembled baboons. He shoved Portia towards his Jeep and pulled a canister of pepper spray from his pocket. One of the creatures tried to run past David on all fours, and David hit it with a stream of cayenne pepper solution. The animal veered off, screaming and pawing at its muzzle. The second baboon went right at David. From his jacket pocket, he pulled an old sap provided by a retired cop David knew. A lucky swing caught the beast alongside its head as it clawed at David, ripping his jacket. The creature sprawled on the pavement of the road, stunned.

"They have my baby," Portia yelled, then started to run back towards the apartment complex. David grabbed her and shoved her through the driver's side open door.

"Stay here, lock the doors," he commanded. From the back, he yanked the antique shotgun from the Jeep's rear and ran towards the buildings. Portia sat crying in the Jeep as Doc yelled over the dropped radio for David. Portia heard two loud reports. Then the pepper-sprayed baboon beast tried to claw its way into the vehicle.

Senior Special Agent Richard Johnson sat looking at the two dead baboon beasts in the coroner's morgue.

"First time I did autopsies on a monkey in the human morgue," said Dr. Michael Speck.

"They're not really baboons, are they?" asked Richard.

"No. They're closer to what anthropologists say are our hominid ancestors. Which I would love to do a scholarly paper on, but you Feds told me I would wind up in federal prison if I did."

"National security," said Richard.

"Humph. Too bad the police had to shoot them."

"Well, Doctor, it was shoot them or have a dead young woman. Let me know when your report is done and I'll pick it up. Do not send anything via email."

Richard had interviewed Portia Strong and her parents with the county sheriff detectives. A physical examination proved Portia had given birth some days before. The apartment complex was seized and sealed off by Federal and State authorities under Hazmat contamination's cover story due to a massive meth lab. No one would push back on that tale as it had happened before on the Peninsula.

The tell-tale evidence of the all too familiar dimensional portal existed in the manager's office and two other apartments. The good news was that authorities found two four-year-old children smuggled in from Mexico. If their parents were found, they would be reunited.

Doc Anderson raised a fuss about how David Mooney was a hero abducted by aliens. Richard shut him up with a carrot and a stick. The federal agents would contact him about any 'weirdness' around Port Angeles. Doc would keep his mouth shut. Simultaneously, people looked for David and Portia's baby. If Doc opened his mouth, he would take a one-way trip to a unique federal facility.

"Doc, he is a hero. We'll keep looking for him." Richard knew that David Mooney was probably residing with a certain blue-skinned woman near and dear to Richard's heart in an alternate reality. He could not tell Doc Anderson that fact.

Things quieted down after a couple of months. Donald had David declared legally deceased as some blood matched David's blood type at the scene. After the memorial service, Jeff went back to the company office; his business was overwhelmed due to the Portia Strong Rescue's positive fallout.

"Just because David was a bit paranoid did not mean he had no reason for the paranoia," Jeff had said at the memorial. "He was a damn fine, hard-working employee and a damn fine person. He is missed."

As Jeff unlocked the main entrance door, he heard something odd. *Is that a baby crying?* he thought. He strode to his office and found the source of the noise. Sitting in a sizeable padded basket was a Black infant. Stuck to the basket with duct tape was a handwritten note:

Here is Portia's son. It took a while, but I found a way. I'll be back after I take care of some things.

P. S. Tell my family and all those people who thought I was nuts; I love my family, but you and all the others can go fuck yourselves. I was right!

FILE 9
THE GENTLEMAN
& THE TIGER

Chapter One

Richard Johnson stood in the large bay at the National Guard Armory in Kitsap County, Washington. Assembled in front of the Senior Special Agent and awaiting his briefing were some hundred federal, state, county, and municipal law enforcement and military personnel. He did not want to be here. However, as the old saying was, ours was not to reason why and so forth and so on.

Richard possessed an in-depth PowerPoint presentation which Homeland Security Investigations Special Agent Kim Kupar and Special Agent Brenna Freiberg of the federal Fish and Wildlife Agency helped create. Kim's husband, Hank Thomas, the big cat expert from the Woodland Park Zoo, sat in the audience as a special advisor. For, the reason for this assembly was an oversized feline. A giant mutated sabretooth cat by the name of Sir Khan was the feline in question.

Richard glanced at Kim. The woman sat stiff and stared straight ahead. She was not happy. Sir Khan and she had a special bond from the first time she had met him. This unique connection led to the hunting cat coming to her aid on two occasions. When someone, even a tiger-cat, saves your life, you remember that fact. Now, she had to capture or kill him. Kim was a professional, but agency loyalty had its limits.

Richard cleared his throat and spoke into the microphone connected to the podium. "Thank you all for coming here. You all have been coffee-ed, donut-ed, and bagel-ed to death, so now it's time for the mission brief."

There was some laughter as the law enforcement types had been through this before. Give everyone some treats and coffee, then tell them what pain in the ass job existed for them.

"The working title for this mission, this project, is Feline Arrest. There is a huge cat out there we need to find, capture, and cage... or kill."

Richard oversaw the hour-long briefing. He watched the incredulous looks on many of the personnel's faces when Kim and Brenna explained Sir Khan's who and what. A sabretooth tiger was a thing of fantasy novels and films, not real life in the Pacific Northwest. The assembled people had to accept that the creature of fantasy and ancient fossil records existed in a modern form. And, those members of this group must find it.

"Well, that is what we have today, ladies and

gentlemen. Your agencies and commands chose you because of your skills and your ability to deal with a dangerous classified project. Make no mistake about this: Sir Khan and his pride are as dangerous as any terrorist organization around when they get their dander up. Us tracking them into their territory in the Olympic National Forest will get their anger up. So, are there any questions?"

A female USAF Pararescue Sergeant stood up. "Master Sergeant Honor Blackman, sir. If these—cats—come at us, we can use our weapons, correct?"

Kim Kupar stood up to answer. "The plan is to use drugged meat, capture nets and tiger pits to get them caged. However, no one has to risk dying. We all want to go home after this is over."

A SWAT member from Kitsap County stood up. "SWAT Sergeant John Cable. Why not just use poison bait?"

Brenna stood up. "Because we do not want a bunch of dead native animals, that is why." Brenna glared a bit at the personnel. "Fish and Wildlife is my purview. Killing a bunch of innocent fauna because of non-native creatures is not something my agency will sanction."

The large Black man sat down, but Richard could tell he did not like Brenna's answer.

"Look-it, guys and gals," Richard said. "This project is not our idea of fun. But we have certain constraints and limitations. We cannot perform slash and burn operations in a national forest used by millions of U.S. and Canadian citizens. Thus, this is the best operation we could develop, which solves with less camage and destruction. We have Native

Americans in the area who do not like some of their traditional lands screwed over. Some would just as soon let the huge cats roam free."

"But they have killed people," someone called out.

"That's right. Our hand was forced. Thus, all of you are here."

There was some muted conversation among the assembled men and women. Richard asked one last time, "Any more questions? Okay, then. Those briefing packets are classified. Do not let the public see them; keep them locked up when not in your personal possession. We will meet back here at O dark thirty tomorrow morning, except for the air units. You will deploy from your airfields. Get some good food and good rest tonight—no late-night drink-fests. You will need all your skills to face Sir Khan. Trust me. I've seen him in action."

After the assembly cleared, Richard walked over to Kim. "Hey, partner, I know you are far from happy with this."

"Yes, but I signed onto this job with my eyes wide open. And I know the danger of a Bengal tiger turned man and woman killer. I helped kill one, remember?"

Kim seemed to be staring at something no one else could see. "Sir Khan did not ask to be created. Some sick humans made him. And know he has reproduced with a local, larger than typical, cougar. His cubs grew and tasted human blood when they killed those Chinese Triad members. It doesn't matter Khan did it to save me or helped us with those blue-skinned humanoids from another universe. What matters is they have killed humans and may not be controllable."

She looked at Richard. "I'll do what I have to do. Just don't expect me to put Sir Khan or his family down." Kim turned and walked away.

"This is hard on her," said Brenna. "I don't like the thought of killing majestic animals like Sir Khan. However, he and his family are now an invasive species, just like those damned flying dragons that got me involved with the Why Files Project. So, I do what I must to keep a balance in nature."

"Huh. We nasty monkeys create the unbalance, then think we can put it all right again," said Richard. "Yeah, right."

Unbeknownst to the assembled military and law enforcement, there was already a group of humans hunting Sir Khan in the big cat's claimed territory. Viktor Mironov had grown up in the U.S. under an assumed name and identity. His great grandparents were the last of a series of Soviet operatives snuck in during Stalin's rule. They raised some good little Soviet sleeper agents who in turn raised Viktor. As far as Viktor knew, his family was the only one who pulled off the whole hidden 'family of spies' routine over three generations. It didn't matter that Stalin led to Khrushchev to Brezhnev to Andropov and eventually to Putin, Viktor's fake family tree extended to some immigrants who fled Russia as Lenin and Stalin killed the Romanovs. They assumed the identities of Good White Russians, who the Allies supported to keep the Bolsheviks from ruling Russia. As the fear of communism grew in the United States, Victor's family's knowledge of Russia and the language landed them

U.S. government jobs. Not even the FBI under Hoover had any idea of the spies right under their noses. Joseph McCarthy's list of Communist Spies in the State Department did not include the Mironovs.

So, Viktor's grandparents secretly supported the Rosenbergs in stealing the atomic secrets, providing aid to Castro's revolution and privately supporting the anti-war movement during Viet Nam. His parents then raised very good little Marxists right under the noses of the U.S. Government. Viktor's brother and two sisters performed more passive roles in supporting the USSR's missions, obtaining jobs in the medical fields and teaching at very liberal universities. On the other hand, Viktor was given knowledge of the family secrets and groomed to be a real spy.

Then the Berlin Wall and the USSR fell. There would be no more support from the Kremlin any time soon.

Viktor was a bit of a savant when it came to foreseeing global problems. Thus, as his parents aged, he contacted Russian Organized Crime before the Warsaw Pact collapsed. The Russian sleeper agent soon demonstrated a ruthlessness that surprised many of the Russian Mafia. Using money skimmed off the Kremlin funds before 1990 (Viktor was a crook even as a teenager), the former Soviet spy became a mover and shaker in the underworld. His contacts with the former KGB agents, many of who began working for the Russian mafia, made him a force to be reckoned with, not to mention people in government who saw him as an ordinary American.

In Viktor's spare time, he also did some hunting and

made contacts with the rarified Big Game community. Thus, when he spread the word around with some money about a new breed of big cats on the Kitsap Peninsula, he found people willing to be part of a semi-authorized hunt. The argument a new invasive species was a pest or varmint open to general killing was persuasive. Especially an invasive species that killed humans.

Viktor looked at the eleven multicultural hunters standing under the high-end camouflage netting at a private residence on the edge of the Olympic National Park. Victor bought the older house a month prior just for this operation. Again, his savant at foreseeing problems raised its head. Viktor's well-developed contacts meant he had no issues obtaining interested parties at a moment's notice.

Besides some professional hunters, part of the group was from the 'dark side.' There were two Chinese Triad members still seeking satisfaction and genetic material due to past casualties from their creation of a sabretooth cat. Three Russian government agents, two of them with a solid background in genetic science, were along to obtain samples of Sir Khan to use in their zoological creations. The third Russian was a stone-cold killer.

The other seven hunters included one semi-famous big game trophy poacher from Africa. The remaining six were well-healed individuals, including one female. Viktor followed the Reservoir Dogs idea and gave each member of the hunt a code name or requested they pick their own. The less everyone knew about each other, the better if things fell apart legally. Of course, the Chinese and Russian operatives demanded secrecy.

Thus, the three Russians were Kildare, Casey and Harding. The Chinese names became Sweet and Sour. The Black African poacher chose Lion. The remaining six were satisfied in color codes like in the Tarantino movie. They became Red, Blue, Green, Brown, Orange, and Pink. The huntress chose Pink.

"Okay, my new friends," Viktor said. "I have split you into two groups with myself in Group One as the leader. Lion will lead Group Two. We agreed to the leadership as twelve of us running through the dense forest willy-nilly will get someone shot, ate or arrested. Any complaints about this at this late date? Good. Lion. You have a question."

"Trophies," asked the muscular African. "Have you created a pathway for us to export our trophies?"

"Of course. You have all paid a premium price for this chance to obtain one-of-a-kind kills. I will ensure each specimen will be taken out without official notice."

"However," Viktor continued, "I have received information that some law enforcement agencies are in the area, possibly because animals killed some Chinese 'tourists.' Thus, we may compete with people using helicopters and the such."

Pink shrugged. "Competition makes success that much sweeter."

"We know how to hide from American authorities," stated Kildare. "Just get us near the requested specimen."

The Siberian Russian known as Harding displayed a feral grin and said nothing.

"You all have your maps and equipment," said Viktor. "Our Russian friends obtained some encoded scrambled radios, so no one should be able to listen in. Use them sparingly. Officials can notice static from a scrambled signal and will wonder who is hiding their transmissions."

The sun was peaking over the horizon.

"Time to move. We have a lot of walking to do."

Early the following day, Richard Johnson watched the various government teams deploy to their sectors. The air units would swoop in after the ground units were well into the forest and mountains. Satellite and high-altitude surveillance drones picked up some possible targets. There was a lot of flora and fauna in the woods under the thick forest canopy. Thus, distinguishing between the various heat sources was difficult. Sir Khan seemed to understand 'eyes in the sky' due to his enhanced intelligence. Richard and Kim both knew his ability to disappear at will.

Richard walked over to Kim and Hank as they checked their packs and equipment. Hank had a heavy-duty tranquilizer rifle and Kim carried her Howdah pistol, which dispatched a Bengal tiger years ago. Richard doubted Kim would be able to use it on Sir Khan or his offspring unless she or Hank were about to be eaten.

"So, you about ready?" Richard asked.

"Yes," replied his investigative partner. "I'm just not happy. I'll follow orders, but the thought of killing Sir Khan when the people he killed were trying to hurt me and others—it just doesn't sit well."

"I know. Khan saved my butt also. Maybe we can catch him and his pride. Miracles do happen."

"We can hope, I guess. Meet you at the SUV."

As Richard walked away, her husband, Hank Thomas, stepped up and hugged Kim. "I've got your back, lover. If we need to steal a big cat or two rather than kill them count me in."

Kim sighed. "If it was just so easy. It's not. I don't want to see you in prison somewhere."

"No chance, I'm too slick."

Kim smiled, then kissed him. "Come on, big man. We might as well get this over."

The married couple met Brenna and Richard at the SUV. Richard drove as he knew the area better. Their four-person team's task was to move on some park service roads and trails up and around Mount Carrie, eventually bouncing around until they neared Mount Olympus, the highest peak in Olympic National Park. Rumors were there was a system of caves known only to some indigenous tribes in history. High altitude imagery and ground-penetrating radar hinted at these, but no one had taken the time or effort to make a thorough examination. Now, if Sir Khan found them, he would lead the law enforcement officials to their discovery.

Some of the units, including those rappelling down from helicopters, were outfitted to stay multiple nights in the wilderness. Richard and company could stay overnight around their SUV. Richard equipped their vehicle with additional communication equipment to act as a command post and an emergency medical site if necessary. The senior special agent had no delusions that this operation would be easy or quick. At the end of one week, he would contact the powers that be and decide if warranted additional time. The next step would be to issue hunting permits and bounties on the feline creatures. That would assuredly lead to a revolt by Kim.

Brenna monitored the government radio as Richard drove slowly; Hank and Kim watched for large animal signs. "SWAT with Sergeant John Cable just repelled in the south of Mount Olympus. They'll work their way north and push anything back to the supposed caverns."

"How about Honor Blackman and her pararescue team?"

"They dropped in the south of Mount Anderson, and well move north also."

"Kim, think the helicopters will make Sir Khan go to ground?"

Kim shrugged. "Maybe. He may have a litter of kittens or two among his group. His mate could be pregnant, and the females of the first litter are well into breeding age."

"Time flies fast when you're having fun," said Hank.

"So, is there a chance our large cat friend could try and lead his pride out and around our units?"

"He is no normal big cat. They are smart enough to present a problem under normal circumstances. Sir Khan has an unusually grasp about the capabilities of the nasty monkeys tracking him. He could surprise us all."

Richard grunted. "I was afraid you'd say that."

V iktor Mironov and his group were a day's march into the
   Olympics when they watched the helicopters drop their
personnel cargo. The three Russians plus Pink and Blue
hunkered down, watching with scopes and binoculars.

"Spetsnaz," said Harding, the killer with a grin.

"Think they saw us?" asked Blue.

"If they did, they would be dropping in on our heads
right now," replied Pink. Viktor assigned the huntress to his
group to watch her and stop any conflicts with the Chinese.
Russians were chauvinistic enough, but these Chinese were
worse. So far, Pink had impressed him with her forest skills.
She was used to working alone, he could tell.

"Our huntress is correct. We just need to watch and
avoid them. They might just push our prey towards us by
accident."

"They have no idea we are here," said Kildare, the
younger of the two doctors. "We could slip in and slit their
throats as they sleep."

"Don't underestimate American Spetsnaz," said
Harding.

"My highly trained comrade is correct," said Viktor.
"Thinking Americans are soft because they have many
creature comforts is wrong. They have many years of combat
experience in Afghanistan and Iraq."

"You fought them in the Mid-East?" Blue asked
Harding. The man gave the American a cold smile.

"Okay, we proceed slowly, still looking for the big cat
sign," said Viktor. "As I said, our American cops could stir our

prey, make it move."

"Or, hunt them," said Pink.

Four hours later, after bouncing up trails more suited for horses, Richard stopped the SUV. The team exited the SUV and stretched. Mount Carrie loomed up in front, with Mount Olympus further to the southwest. The forest was thick and damp, even with the spring weather.

"Looks like another world, doesn't it?" said Brenna.

"This is your stomping grounds, isn't it?" asked Hank.

"Yep. Lots of flora and fauna, lots of quiet. I've spent many an overnight out here, looking for illegal hunters, loggers, and pot farms. I never thought I'd be looking for a sabretooth cat and his pride."

Kim stepped off the primitive trail and stood still. After no movement for a minute, Richard moved near her.

"See something?"

"He's out there, Richard. He saw us approach, sensed us. I… sense him."

"Sir Khan knows we want him?"

She looked at Richard. "Of course. We made Sir Khan. He understands us nasty monkeys just fine."

SWAT Sergeant John Cable led his eleven-person team through the thick forest. People did not understand that a large part of the Olympic area was a rainforest—some military units trained in the summer months before deploying to Earth's jungle areas. His father was a Viet Nam veteran and told him about jungle operations. Now he knew about what his dad experienced.

The team moved as quietly as possible. Simultaneously, a couple of experienced hunters in the group checked for the large feline sign.

"That's a big mountain," said officer Kaminski.

"Just hope we don't have to climb it."

"These tigers hang out there, Sergeant?"

"That's the report. Now, quiet, watch and listen."

A sizeable tawny shape shadowed the twelve humans. For a creature so large, the offspring of Sir Khan moved like a shadow. The smell of the two-legs was familiar but not one of usual prey. However, the strange feline knew they were a threat to her sire and the others. If she could chase them from the area, she would.

Chief Master Sergeant Honor Blackman pushed her group of pararescue personnel through the thick forest. The plan was to climb partway up onto Mount Anderson and set up a lookout and listening post. The military had provided some high-tech sensors and ground-based anti-personnel radar units for surveillance. The government tested the equipment over the years on the Southwest Border and in Europe. Honor and her team had lots of practice with the equipment and were quite confident in its use.

On they went as the sun climbed and then sank on the horizon. They could have been dropped on the mountain by their helicopter. However, that would destroy the idea of disturbing the feline creatures and driving them to their hidey holes. Some anesthetic gas in a cave was the preferred method of capture. If not, the military members would shoot them.

Just before dark, Honor called the team to a halt in a good spot. "Let's get set up, people," Honor directed. "We may cause our targets to move around so we can find them."

An hour later, the camp was set up, with monitoring teams in place. Those not on shift Honor told to get some rest. "We are about to have a hectic time."

Darkness fell; the camp was quiet, other than the slight buzzing sound from the surveillance equipment. Just as the military personnel surveilled the area for their feline targets, a set of oversized cat-eyes watched them.

"I think I have something, Chief," a Senior Airman called out. Honor was at the computer screen in a flash.

"Seems to be a large moving heat source."

"A deer, Chief?"

"Look at it with the FLIR."

The FLIR scope showed something lithe and staring back at them. Then the creature was gone.

"That was no deer. We have contact."

Richard was dozing in the SUV driver's seat. Driving up and down small trails until they became stuck seemed like the last thing to do. Brenna smacked his shoulder to wake him up.

"Contact."

"Where?"

"On the slopes of Mount Anderson. Blackman's crew picked up a large cat on their FLIR."

"None from any of the teams walking in or on the surrounds roads?"

"Nope."

"It's a scout," interjected Kim. "One of the younger pride members sensed something strange and checked it out. He or she will report to Sir Khan."

"Really?" asked Richard. "His pride is that sophisticated?"

"Think of super lions, super wolves in a pack. They have ways to communicate danger."

Richard sat in thought for a moment. "I take it going out at night to track them is not smart?" he asked.

"Unless you want to goad them into trying to exterminate us with extreme prejudice, no."

"They own the night for real," added Hank. "We play with it with technology. Big cats' senses work a lot better than ours when the sun goes down."

"Okay. So, send the word out. Everyone camp in place and wait. We move at sunrise."

Officer Smyth walked out into the dark to take a piss. He grumbled to himself about having to go further out as there were females as part of the SWAT team, so he didn't offend anyone.

"Bullshit," he mumbled as he started to unzip. Everything went black as a large shape flattened him.

"Where's Smyth?" asked Sergeant Cable some ten minutes later.

"He went to take a piss," someone called out, followed by some suppressed titters.

"Find him, goddammit! Pararescue reported a contact. One cat means two, means three. Find him!"

Cable reported Smyth missing to all the other units. People checked their weapons, no longer thought of sleep—there was an assassin in the night.

Sergeant Cable wanted to do a night search but knew it could result in more missing or dead. Richard Johnson was correct in telling everyone to stay in place. All Cable could do was sit and grind his teeth.

Viktor and Lion's groups sat in cold camps, no fires. Not only did they not want to tip off the saber-cats (nickname someone created), but there were law enforcement types in the forest also. Viktor sat down next to Pink and passed her a flask. The huntress took it, sniffed it, then took a swig.

"I have a question," Pink whispered.

"Shoot, but not me."

"Do all people of Russian descent drink Vodka?"

"Yes. It dulls the pain of the horrible weather in Russia."

"But you were born and grew up in America."

"But I am still Russian at heart."

Pink glanced around at the dark. "So, we are about halfway between Mount Olympus and Mount Anderson."

"Yes. Hopefully, the law enforcement personnel—"

"Psst. Viktor." It was Casey.

"Yes?"

"A frequency we have a scrambled key code for—just heard on it a cop is missing."

Viktor smiled. "Now the fun really begins."

Sergeant Cable organized a search at first light. They found the unconscious but battered Smyth in the low branches of a tree.

"Leopards stash prey in the trees to keep it from other predators," said Hank. "The man is lucky to be alive."

"Not really," said Kim "Sir Khan's offspring are not true maneaters. They kill for a reason, not just to eat."

"You're giving Sir Khan some high levels of intelligence, Kim," said Richard.

"Humans created him and gave him superior intelligence. That is a fact. His offspring inherited some of it."

"Well, time to buckle down and get this done. I'm sending some of the other patrols towards Cable and Blackman. We do a triangle from Mount Olympus, Anderson, and Carrie, where you say you sensed Sir Khan. There are cats inside this triangle. Someplace is their hidey-hole."

Sir Khan knew he and his pride needed to evade the tall monkeys hunting them. His scouts communicated to him the creatures' locations and activities. The female known to him as Silver due to her unique coloring had disabled one of the hunters, treated it as prey. Now, the monkeys were agitated. However, in his unusual intelligence, Sir Khan knew conflict was unavoidable unless he found a secure den.

Low growls heard for miles with the offspring's superior hearing called them to assemble at a specific cavern. Sir Khan found a year prior connected system of tunnels and caves formed by some ancient glaciation with a touch of ocean uplift volcanism. Even the Native American tribes didn't know the extent of the caves. However, Sir Khan sensed the monkeys' machines and understood the hiding place must be deep to avoid detection.

The giant feline raised his head and sniffed. She was among the monkeys, the humans who hunted him. Why the one he saved was chasing him confused the Sabretooth Cat Plus. The special connection between him and Kim was not enough to keep his pride safe. Sir Khan growled and grumbled as he accepted the distasteful fact; all humans were a threat, even the Tiger Lady.

Sir Khan was on the move, his pregnant oversized female cougar mate following him. A great pregnant cat was not as helpless as a pregnant Homo sapiens. Thus, the two made good time towards their special place near Mount Olympus. A half dozen offspring would join the Alpha pair there. With another litter of cats, Sir Khan's species would be on the way to sustainability in numbers. Humans may consider them as an invasive new species; Sir Khan just looked at them as family. Woe to any animal which dares to challenge the new Apex Predator.

Drone contact," called out Brenna as she steadied the computer uplink with the surveillance machine. Modern technology meant Richard did not have to request helicopter or aircraft flyovers from the Customs and Border Protection Aviation Branch. Some three drones were crisscrossing the Olympics, with a satellite on loan from the U.S. Military about to pass over. Eventually, any large animals moving would be detected.

"What do we have, Brenna?" asked Richard.

"One to two creatures moving fast to the southern slopes of Mount Olympus." The Fish and Wildlife agent then frowned. "I also have some indications of some possible humans heading that direction."

"Ours?"

"No. But well camouflaged with some heat-dissipating clothing, it seems."

"Military surplus tech?"

"Could be. But Cable's group is the closest, and it isn't them. We have an unknown bogie."

"Aw shit. All we need are some hikers in the way."

"Richard, I think we have some competition," interjected Kim.

"What do you mean, Kim?"

"Sir Khan saved me from the Chinese Triad. They are not noted for accepting failure or defeat easily."

"Aw, double shit. Pass it to the field units. We have possible two-legged hostiles added to the four-legged ones."

Viktor and Lion's groups traveled separated by over a mile of the forest but headed in the same direction. Casey had managed to hack into a drone's circuit and saw the images of the creatures moving towards Mount Olympus. However, the law enforcement types moved in a trail of the targets also.

"Where are the military types?" whispered Viktor.

"A couple of klicks to our east. They may bump into

Lion before us."

"Give him a short heads up on the scrambled frequency." Viktor turned towards the others in his group. "Danger close, people. Cats and humans," he whispered.

Pink walked up to him. "I do better solo. Mind if I forge ahead? If I get caught, I'll keep them busy with female bullshit."

Viktor grinned. He could tell Pink could use her femineity to the best advantage and distract even other women. "It's your funeral. Remember, there are hunting cats out there."

Pink grinned back. "Pussy hunting pussy. Who'd of thought?"

Sergeant Cable pushed his remaining nine SWAT members hard. He sent one man back with the injured Smyth and could not send one of two female members without being yelled at by his supervisors. Once he had received the drone's images, he knew his team had to intercept, one way or another. He didn't worry about stealth. Cable wanted speed. He moved up and down the unit, checking and counterchecking.

There was a cry of alarm and Cable heard some cracking of brush. Cable sprinted forward towards the sounds. Hanging upside down in a tree on a snare line was male officer Klein.

"What the...! Cut him down!" Cable yelled. "Fan out, three sixty degrees coverage. A big cat did not set that snare; a human did."

Sixty seconds later, one of his female officers yelled a challenge at an unseen person. Cable moved towards the officer and saw a face as dark as his emerge from the brush.

"I am so sorry. My name is Abraham Bello. I am with a group from the University of Washington trying to trap a specimen of a large feline we heard exists in the national park. We did not mean—"

"Put your hands up and walk towards me," ordered Cable. "Who in the fu—"

Another officer yelled out a challenge, someone spoke in Mandarin Chinese, and all hell broke loose. Bullets began to fly in every direction.

The gunfire echoed through the Olympic National Forest. Richard began yelling over the radio, trying to get an answer. Chief Blackman came up on the radio net saying her team was en route to support.

"Goddammit, who is doing all the shooting?"

"It's like I said," interjected Kim. "We have some competition to get to Sir Khan. We need to get to Mount Olympus. Now!"

Richard cursed under his breath then looked at Brenna, Hank, and Kim. "Okay, who here is uncomfortable with repelling from a Blackhawk?"

Viktor led the remainder of his group towards the south face of Mount Olympus. He cursed to himself as the gunfire would indeed send any big cats running. Pink had disappeared into the forest as if she lived here. If she successfully took a trophy, getting an even dead specimen of the creature, this project would not be a total bust. Viktor was more than willing to arrange a sharing of biological samples to make as many people happy as possible.

The gun battle lasted a good quarter-hour which told Viktor that Lion and his group was probably dead or under arrest. Because the Russian-American had kept people from knowing each other's personal information, anyone arrested could pass on only limited data. Viktor had purchased the meeting house under an assumed name so that item would lead to a dead-end. He just needed to get out of the forest unnoticed.

Viktor halted the four remaining group members for a quick powwow.

"Decision time, gentlemen," he said in a soft voice, "do we continue knowing the authorities are on our trail, or do we continue, hoping to take a specimen?"

Casey, Kildare and Harding all said 'go.' Blue, as the remaining civilian hunter, hesitated.

"I can hire some high-end lawyers if I get caught, but with the gun battle—"

"You'll have to make it back on your own, Blue."

"I can do that. I am not a stranger to jungles or forests. Let me take a whizz, and then you can point me in a good direction."

Harding sneered as Blue stepped into the brush to do his business. "Bring only military next time," he hissed.

Blue was zipping up when Sir Khan's offspring slid out of the bushes, latched his jaws around the man's throat and yanked him deeper into the forest. Harding saw the brush move and was up, aiming his weapon at the spot Blue had pissed.

"It has him," Harding said in a whisper.

"Shit. Three sixty coverage, gentlemen," said Viktor.

The four Russians stood back-to-back, looking for a threat. When nothing appeared in five minutes, Viktor said, "Now what?"

"We go on," said Kildare. "A specimen is close."

Viktor shrugged. "Okay. Slow and by the numbers. They are stalking us."

The CBP Blackhawk pilot was good. He landed in a clearing down from Mount Carrie, picked up the three Agents and one Zoologist, and swung out towards Mount Olympus. Crew chief on board hooked the four up with the repelling gear; then, he picked a snowfield on the southeast side of the mountain.

"Get out and down ASAP," said the pilot. "There are a lot of odd up and downdrafts around these mountains."

"Roger that," said Richard. "I'll go first. You can follow me or drop off the other side."

A minute later, Richard was on the edge of the snowfield. He unhooked and walked a few yards, looking for any moving snow. Avalanches were not out of the question on Mount Olympus with its glaciers and all. Brenna and Hank repelled down on the starboard side of the 'copter. Kim was halfway down the port side when it happened. An odd and forceful downdraft came off the mountain slopes, slapped the helicopter and sent it twisting away. Kim's rope slung her out and away from the selected snowfield.

"Fuck!" yelled Richard as he watched helplessly. The pilot regained control a mile distance. Kim took no chances and dropped between two large trees, hit and rolled. Somehow, she unhooked from the rope, and the pilot swung the Blackhawk out and away from the mountain.

"You okay, Kim?" Richard called on the radio.

"Yes. Stay there, and I'll come to you."

Kim heard a familiar cough from behind her. Slowly she turned, her hand on her pistol. Hank had the capture gun.

Staring at her was a huge cougar/tiger mix. It was not Sir Khan but looked to be one of the cats which rescued her from the Triad Agents months back. The sabretooth-mix stared at her for a moment, then turned and disappeared into the forest.

"I have contact. Come to me," called out Kim. "Follow my tracks. I need to follow one of Sir Khan's kids."

"Wait for us, dammit," called out Richard.

"No time. There is a den nearby; I can feel it."

Richard cursed as Kim cut the radio connection. "Damn, she is stubborn."

"Tell me about it," said her husband, Hank.

Kim made her way through slackening snow and wound her way through the trees. The cat tracks were easy to follow. Judging by how the big cat seemed to be on a mission, Kim surmised he stopped en route to the den. Kim saw a set of large male testicles as it lifted its tail to move and wondered how many sisters he had. When Sir Khan rescued her near Port Angeles, she saw the offspring fleetingly as they took out the Triad kidnappers. People still had trouble believing the huge mutant tiger saved her, but Kim knew the truth. The sabretooth cat, which she had just seen, must have remembered her scent and determined she was no threat. Hank, Richard and Brenna, how they were viewed was the question.

Kim worked her way through the sloped trees and patches of snow. Mount Olympus was well known for its snowfall and glaciers, not for caverns. Yet, Sir Khan had found some den that kept him from modern surveillance. However, because people died in rescuing Kim, he and his pride became criminals. If Kim could just find them first, maybe she could find a way to keep them alive and free.

Pink moved quickly and silently. No one expected a woman who looked like a fashion model to be a world-class hunter and a predator. Just turned thirty, Pink already had half a dozen significant hunts under her belt with a room full of trophy heads. A sabretooth cat head would look good next to her male lion trophy.

She shifted the .338 Lapua built on an AR-15 beefed-up frame on her shoulder. Pink had her personally designed quick-release sling, which enabled her to bring into action in the blink of an eye. Pink liked the high-velocity round over traditional oversized big game rounds used in conventional African safari elephant guns. The hollow point bullet would expand to immense size when it hit the dense body of the giant cat. There may be some pelt damage, but Pink had a friend taxidermist who could do wonders.

The woman known as Pink sensed and saw something large move quickly through the fir trees up ahead. She unslung her rifle and used the scope to surveil the woods.

"All right," she whispered. "A big cat."

The feline had silver tints to its tawny coat. Pink moved forward in a combat crouch and re-established the sight picture. The sabretooth froze in its path and looked directly at Pink. The huntress knew she had been noticed and would have to take the shot. Pink let out her breath and began to squeeze the rifle's trigger.

Something slammed into Pink's back and the rifle boomed. The bullet went wide, and the big cat melted into the forest. Pink stumbled around and regained her balance.

"Federal agent. Drop your rifle."

Kim stood with her pistol pointed at the unknown woman.

"You always sneak up behind people and smack them?" asked Pink.

"When they're part of an illegal hunt, interfering with a law enforcement operation, yes. Now, drop your rifle."

"How about I lay it down? It costs more than you make in a week." Pink began to bend over slowly.

A large feline head appeared behind the huntress's left shoulder, and Kim's eyes shifted to it. Pink saw the momentary distraction and seized the opportunity. The brunette launched the rifle like a spear, then leapt after it. This was a chance to escape and Pink would not let it pass. The rifle barrel struck Kim's Glock and almost knocked it from her hand. In a flash, Pink was grappling with Kim for control of the pistol.

Had Pink known Kim's background, she would not have tried a physical fight. The next thing Pink realized, she saw stars and was lying on her back.

"Well, young lady, now you have added a charge of assault on a Federal Agent to your court time. Do you want to try something else?"

"What the hell was that?"

"East Indian martial arts called *kalaripayattu*. Now, roll over so I can slap the handcuffs on you."

Kim's blood froze when she heard the tiger cough from behind her.

"My rifle," Pink said.

"Stay still," replied Kim. The federal agent slowly turned around at looked at the young saber-cat. The silver-tinted fur shined in the sunlight as the giant feline looked into Kim's eyes. Sir Khan's oversized genes were breeding true. If these saber-cats kept producing, there was a distinct possibility that the Olympic Peninsula's ecology would never be the same.

The feline sniffed at Kim and took a step forward. The special agent knew she might kill the large cat with her handgun, but only after the predator killed her and possibly the huntress. In one fluid motion, the creature seemed to have a change of heart, turned and leapt back into the underbrush.

It took a moment for Kim to realize she still had a violent subject to control. As the raven-haired Kim turned towards Pink, the brunette slammed into her, knocking her to the forest floor. Pink tried to bite Kim's gun hand as she wrestled for the pistol. Kim screamed in anger and stuck her freehand thumb in Pink's right eye. Pink yelped and stopped biting as she twisted her head away from Kim's painful jab. She scissored her legs around Pink's upper torso and levered her to the ground. Kim managed to holster her pistol as she used her strong thigh muscles to squeeze the breath out of the hunter.

Pink fought dirty and tried to punch the female agent in her crotch. Kim responded by loosening her leg scissors and lashing out with her booted feet into Pink's substantial breasts. Pink cried out in pain and tried to roll away, then stand up. In seconds Kim had Pink in an armbar and levered face down in the dirt.

Kim painfully twisted the hunter's right arm and wrist until she clicked a handcuff on it. "Keep fighting, bitch, and I'll snap your wrist, then break your fingers."

"Okay, okay, I give."

"Give me your other wrist."

Kim clicked the other handcuff on, then yanked Pink to her feet. "What's your name?"

"Today, it's Pink."

"Wiseass, I see. Well, fingerprints will tell the tale. Now march."

Kim shoved her towards the direction the saber-cat went. She picked up Pink's rifle as they walked into the brush.

"You're not going to take me in now?"

"No. Sir Khan and his pride are on the verge of being

shot all to Hell. They are more important than you. I'll take the heat if you're injured."

Richard, Brenna, and Hank tried to locate Kim as they hustled towards her last know location. Richard tried her on the radio, but Kim did not answer.

"If she is close to Sir Khan and company," said Hank, "she might have turned her radio off."

"Great. So, we stumble through the forest and look for Kim or the cat's sign. Someone used a large caliber weapon and I hope the bullet wasn't meant for Kim."

"It was for one of the cats," said Brenna. "The assholes who snuck in want a specimen or a trophy, maybe both."

"They might not think twice then to shoot one of us," replied Richard.

"Well, we shoot them first, then."

Hank looked at the two Special Agents with a grim expression. "I came to capture big cats, not shoot humans."

"Sometimes Murphy's Law prevails," replied Richard. "Let's get a move on."

Viktor moved his group as fast as he could while keeping a lookout for drones and law enforcement. He no longer worried about an ambush by one of the saber-cats. All the shooting from the firefight would make even the nastiest predator go to ground. The Russian sleeper agent wondered how many of Lion's group survived. Well, at least the troublesome Chinese were out of the picture.

His group was down to four Russians. Viktor knew they were the toughest of the tough; not some trophy hunters used to organized safaris and friendly hotels in between shooting animals while backed up by a professional guide. If anyone could find and take one of the super felines, it would be them.

Pink had not checked in since Victor heard her large caliber weapon discharge. She was either dead or in law enforcement custody. Either way, she was of no further use.

"Activity, Viktor," said Kildare in a near whisper. "Everyone is closing in on Mount Olympus."

The forest and surrounding ground were beginning to slope upwards onto the mountain proper. Victor had hoped any den or hiding places of the large cats would be far from the summit and the glaciers, such as Blue Glacier. Was it not for all the government activity, Viktor initially believed they could have picked up a game trail at the lower levels, even with thickened brush and trees.

"If wishes were horses, beggars could ride," Viktor mumbled.

"Okay," he said in a subdued voice in English. "We find a place to hide and wait for all the cops and soldiers to pass us. Lion's shootout has them all on edge, no Russian speaking if someone is in earshot. If they stumble onto us, get ready to ditch your weapons and play stupid dumb tourist hikers. You all have the fake passports and visas I provided. Understand?"

The three Russians nodded affirmatively.

"Think we can still find a specimen?" asked Casey.

"I think the Americans will drive one or more of the

saber-cats into us. If somehow Sir Khan and all his pride are trapped in the den, then we try to intercept a recovery party coming off the mountain. I am all for stealing a body or live specimen after the Americans do all the work; they will not expect it."

"Sly," said the killer Harding. "I can take them out quietly."

"Hope we don't have to resort to that, my friend. Violence and bodies will result in a different type of hunt; a manhunt, for us."

Kim shoved Pink in front of her as the crude path they were on sloped upward.

"You could uncuff me, so I have better balance," said Pink.

"And have you try to punch me in my lady parts again? I think not."

"I give you my word—"

"Yeah, right. I don't even know your real name, yet I am supposed to trust you."

"My real name is Sally McShane."

"Says you. I'll wait, Miss Pink, until I get the fingerprint results back."

Something significant dislodged loose rock up ahead.

"Freeze," whispered Kim. Whatever was in front heard their talking and knew their location exactly. Kim slid Pink's .338 Lapua rifle off her shoulder. As much as she didn't want to shoot, she also did not want to be killed by an enraged saber-cat or grizzly. Kim stood silently with Pink, the sound of her heart pounding filling her ears.

There was a deep cough behind her, and once again, Kim's blood ran cold. These tiger-related felines were experts at sneaking up on Kim, then coughing to let them know they were near. Kim slowly turned around the rifle at low ready. If it was Sir Khan and she was not overly aggressive, she may not have to shoot.

Something big knocked her over, then Kim felt the raspy tongue of a big cat. She dropped the rifle and hugged Sir Khan.

"Nice to see you too, Big Fella," Kim said with tears in her eyes.

"I don't fucking believe it," Kim heard Pink say.

Kim let Sir Khan nuzzle her some more as she scratched his ears. Then she gently pushed him back so she could stand up. "Pink, meet Sir Khan. Man's attempt at a modern sabretooth cat, but with some additions."

"Like what?" asked Pink.

"High intellect. If Sir Khan had opposable thumbs, we'd really be in the shits." Kim glared at the hunter. "And you wanted a trophy head from one of these fantastic beasts. You should be ashamed."

Pink stared at Sir Khan, who stared back.

"I think your friend here could have killed me at any time," Pink said with a quiver in her voice.

"He was supposed to kill me when we first met," replied Kim. "He chose not to as he felt something for me. Now we have a connection. Some locals claim he is my totem animal."

Kim looked the great beast in his oversized cat's eyes. "We need to get you hidden until we figure something out."

As if to answer, Sir Khan moved past Kim and Pink, stopped, turned around and stared at the two women.

"I think he wants us to follow him," said Pink.

"Now you're learning," replied Kim.

Richard tried to call Kim on the radio and cursed when there was no answer.

"Come on, Richard," said Brenna. "We can track her, catch up. We know she's heading upslope on Mount Olympus. You could call the Blackhawk back."

"No. That big bird could scatter the saber-cats more than they are already. Not to mention the other unknown hunters in the area we need to catch."

Richard looked at Hank. "I am sorry I got you and Kim in this mess."

"Sir Khan is the reason we are here," replied the big cat expert. "Humans have to come to an arrangement with his kind."

"Which right now is kill or catch," said Richard. "Just great. Khan saved my ass also. I keep hoping Kim can help me in keeping him alive and free."

Richard shook his head and cursed some more. "Well, me standing here bitching is solving nothing. Come on. Let's catch up to Kim."

Viktor's group managed to hack into the law enforcement communication network and learned

Sergeant Cable's SWAT team was tied up with Lion and one survivor from that group, plus a couple of wounded SWAT members. Honor Blackman and others were hot-footing to close the circle around Mount Olympus while looking for other 'hunters' and the saber-cats.

"We have a gap in the circle," said Viktor. "Time to push through it.

Some high winds cut down drone usage and the helicopters were being reserved for further transport, especially wounded. The U.S. Government had a Men in Black unit in reserve but would only call these personnel in if things went utterly sour and bizarre. Little did those involved knew things were about to be just that: Sour and bizarre.

Sir Khan kept his pace slow enough so Kim and Pink could keep up with him in the rough and rocky area. The trio moved quickly and quietly through the woods on the slope of Mount Olympus. Kim hoped the big cat's den or hidey-hole was not close to the summit and glacier area. Cold and wet was not fun.

As if reading her mind, Sir Khan stopped some fifty yards in front of the two humans. As soon as they caught up, the feline seemed to disappear into an outcropping of rock. Kim followed him into the gap between a shelf of rock dragging Pink with her. Kim took out her tactical flashlight and followed Sir Khan down an oddly-shaped tunnel. Some seventy-five yards in, the tunnel opened up into a large cavern hewed from solid rock. Her flashlight revealed several saber-cats laying around with what could only be the oversized cougar mother off to one side on a bed of ferns. Sir Khan took good care of his Mother Queen.

"What kind of formation is this?" asked an incredulous Pink.

"Not volcanic. The Olympics are not volcanic."

"The walls looked almost... artificially made."

"Well, whatever. Sir Khan has found his hidey-hole. However, enough people hiking around here could mean someone will stumble on it." Kim looked at the huntress. "And I can't let you go until I ensure Sir Khan and his family are safe from being euthanized or treated like lab rats for the rest of their lives."

Pink looked at Kim. "So, I need to be—silenced."

"Oh, not that way. I am not an assassin, nor will I let these saber-cats hurt innocent people. The Triad members they killed—they deserved death." Kim sat down on a boulder. "Let me puzzle this out. There has to be a solution."

"Well, Agent, you'd better hurry. Your friends will be looking for you."

Richard, Brenna and Hank saw the huge feline pug marks mixed in with Kim's and another person's boot prints.

"Female-sized boots, or a smaller man," said Brenna.

"So, Kim has a prisoner," said Richard.

"Probably from the same people the SWAT ran into and shot up."

"With Sir Khan. I recognize his tracks," interjected Hank.

Richard looked at the trail for a while, then spoke.

"Well, shit. We have to follow and make contact. Hopefully, Kim can keep Sir Khan's brood from eating us."

A s the three began to move up the trail, Viktor's group was some one hundred yards downslope. The Siberian known in the group as Harding whispered to Viktor.

"I catch up and slit their throats. No problem."

Viktor Mironov paused, then said, "Do it."

Fifteen minutes later, as the two agents and the zoologist paused on the trail, looking up at the rocky area ahead, Harding crept closer. The three stood bunched up, which precluded Harding from sneaking up and slicing their throats one at a time. The Siberian carefully slid a Makorav pistol from under his camouflaged jumpsuit. From a pocket, he took a sound suppressor and carefully screwed it onto the pistol barrel. Harding then slowly crept closer.

The male saber-cat appeared from seemingly nowhere. The predator clamped his sabretooth-equipped jaw on the neck of the human, crushing and puncturing it all at once. The pistol clattered on some rocks as the Siberian Russian died.

Richard sensed something and turned to look down the trail they were on just as a large caliber rifle spoke. Kildare had been watching the Siberian through his scope and saw the feline attack. As his fellow Russian died, he fired.

"Fuck!" Richard yelled and swung his MP-5 up as a second thirty caliber round from the Russian Dragunov semi-auto zipped by their heads. He fired a burst down the trail. He knew they had found the rest of the people who had tangled with the SWAT team. Brenna cursed in Norwegian and brought up her shotgun and sent a slug round downrange. Hank readied the capture gun but knew it was for zoo animals, not gunfights.

Sir Khan flew from the cavern before Kim knew what happened. Her human ears did not hear the gunshots but knew something was afoot.

"Stay here, Pink. Don't move."

Pink stared in the near darkness at the big cats in the cavern as they stood up.

Viktor cursed at Kildare for firing but now knew it was too late to call the bullets back. He jumped behind a tree for cover as Casey began shooting using a locally obtained M1A. The thirty caliber rounds slammed into the rocks and wood near Richard and Company. The three ducked down behind trees and rocks.

As Casey raised from cover to fire again, a wounded male saber-cat slammed into him. The man's rifle went flying from the impact as a massive clawed paw took the Russian's face off. Kildare fired into the feline from point-blank range, and the creature collapsed. Viktor turned and clambered back down the trail.

Kildare reloaded his rifle with a fresh magazine. As he raised his head from cover to search for a target, Sir Khan's massive paw shattered his jaw, broke his neck, and cracked his skull. As the dead Russian slumped over, the sabretooth cat dashed down the trail.

Viktor thought he had outdistanced the violence. He

did not sign on for gunfights with federal agents. Viktor always left the violence to others; he was the brains, the savant behind the scene. Thus, it came as an instant surprise when Sir Khan dashed his brains out all over the Olympic National Forest.

Chief Blackman was pushing her people hard when she heard the shooting.

"Double-time, people! We are Pararescue, and some people need our firepower. Move!"

Moments later, a new sound reverberated around the rocky crags of Mount Olympus. The vibrating roar of a hunting sabretooth cat, a sound from prehistory, told everyone an Apex Predator had exacted vengeance.

Kim found Richard, Brenna and Hank near the body of the saber-cat. The son of Sir Khan had died quickly while free, not in a cage.

Hank crushed her in his arms. "Please don't take off like that again," he whispered in her ear. "If I lost you…"

A loud cough, followed by a deep vibrating growl, drew everyone's attention. Sir Khan approached in a hunting crouch with blood on his muzzle and chest. Kim pushed herself from Hank and stepped in front of the enormous tiger-cat's path.

"Sir Khan. No. It's me. Remember? Kim. The Tiger Lady."

The feline stopped and sniffed. Then looked at Richard.

"Hey, big fellow. Remember me? You crushed my

French doors."

Sir Khan paused. He turned and leapt into the brush.

"He's heading back to his den."

Richard looked up the trail. "Kim, we have to go up there and look. In an hour, a whole crapload of people with guns is going to be here. Unless we can figure out a way to capture Sir Khan and his pride, they will die on this mountain."

"They will die in cages. Or in some horrible lab, being dissected for their genetic material."

Richard sighed. "Show me the den; then we can put our heads together."

The four humans made their way back to the hidden cavern. Pink had managed to free herself from the handcuffs but sat scratching the female with silver highlighted fur ears.

"They didn't eat me," the huntress said with a smile.

"Maybe they should have if they realized you were after a trophy," said Kim. "Now what?"

"Good question," replied Richard. "You are going to have some explaining—"

The cave wall began displaying a bluish shimmering which was all too familiar to Kim and Richard.

"Goddammit, not here!" yelled Richard. An all-to-familiar figure sipped through the light. The bluish-purple-skinned female smiled at Richard and Kim.

"Ariya," Richard said through gritted teeth. "Why are you and how are you here?"

"I made this cave for them; to save them."

"Why?" asked Kim. "You are just going to draw the Skara after you. They will kill them."

Ariya shook her head. "No. I have learned how not to be bothered. I've found—a new place. The one you call Sir Khan can come and live there. I will be there to make sure he and his children are well and taken care of for their entire lives."

"Why?" asked Richard as Pink, Brenna and Hank stood with incredulous looks on their faces. Hank and Brenna knew some of the stories, but this was spinning off into new strangeness.

"I love you, Richard. I always will. What I have done is to help you and your friends. And, Sir Khan is like-me. Someone made him what he is, did not ask him if he wanted to be a normal tiger or one which is... different."

Sir Khan stood near his pride. Kim saw the strangeness in his eyes which said he could never just be a tiger. He was a mutated cat with no other family other than what he produced from his loins. Sir Khan was the first of his kind, but not from normal evolution. Nasty monkey humans had tried to turn him into an 'it' rather than just a normal tiger.

"Do it, Ariya," said Kim. "Do it, and I will forever be indebted to you."

"I'm sorry I hurt Richard, your dear friend. Please forgive me." Ariya looked at Richard. "Maybe someday, you can come to where Sir Khan and I will be."

"Take him," Richard said. "Please. Now. Before it is too late."

Ariya nodded and blinked back tears. She made a strange whistling sound, and the saber-cats went through the doorway into another reality. They must have done this before as there was no hesitation.

Sir Khan head-butted Kim and he received the last ear scratch as she cried. Then he leapt through the shimmering doorway and was gone.

Kim sobbed as Hank held her. She saw a best friend leave, maybe never to return.

"What did I just witness?" asked Pink.

"Something you will have to be quiet about," said Brenna. "Or you will be locked away in some dark dungeon never to see the light of day. Or maybe you will disappear." Brenna grunted. "Just hope you never have to deal with any flying, flame-spitting tiny dragons."

The one dead saber-cat allowed a modified cover story. The deceased foreign agents added to it, so there was a reason why no one caught all the saber-cats. LION, aka Bello, and another hunter did time in prison for some federal and state wildlife-related crimes; Bello was then deported. The Men in Black showed up for debriefs and took the saber-cat carcass away. Intelligence agencies claimed other foreign entities spirited away some of the pride. Rumors spread that others were seen up and down the coast.

No one mentioned Ariya.

No one mentioned Pink.

Hank and Kim laid in bed together days later. Hank kissed his wife and said, "Sir Khan will always be missed. He was unique."

"Some evil people created him for bad acts, and he

turned out to be a force for good," replied Kim. "He saved Richard and me."

"Which I am forever grateful," said Hank.

Kim looked at her husband. "You know, maybe it's time to start our own pride. What do ya think?"

Richard took some time off and sat at home watching old science fiction movies. There was a knock on his door, and he went to answer it. Standing at the door was this brunette who looked more like a model than a former trophy hunter.

"Hi. Sally McShane here. I heard you like old sci-fi movies."

"Guilty as charged. But sometimes the truth is stranger than fiction."

"I have some pizza and beer and a hankering to talk about things I can't mention without going to a dungeon."

Richard grinned.

"Come in, Pink. No anchovies, I hope."

FILE 10
MOBY DICK

"Captain Ahab would just love me," Kim Kupar groaned out as she once again made her way to the bathroom. She now knew where the expression "beached whale" originated. Some pregnant woman carrying twins coined the phrase, certainly.

As she finished relieving herself and stood up, one of the twins kicked out hard. "Hey. Whoever did that; quit it. You're beating your mother to death."

The experienced federal special agent made her way back to the ranch-style home's living room to try again to find a comfortable reclining position on the oversized and overstuffed sofa. Since her eighth month, Kim had been on unpaid maternity leave as her ever-growing stomach made it too difficult to work in the office. It was bad enough not to be able to do any investigative fieldwork and be tied to a desk. Now, she was stuck at home with nothing to do but stare at The Boob Tube and feel her unborn kick her insides. The taller than the average black-haired woman, Kim was used to being physically active and fit. Now she felt like a tree sloth in her movements.

"Stop feeling sorry for yourself, woman," Kim loudly said to the empty house. Now was the time she missed Sir Kahn and his ilk. A brilliant beast returned her love, protected her from all threats, and made a tremendous large furry pillow. Once again, Kim thought about getting a large dog. Something like a Great Pyrennes, a dog used to live with and protect a herd or pack of animals. A dog would never replace a man-made saber-tooth cat, but it would provide a decent level of companionship while her husband Hank Thomas worked at Woodland Park Zoo, helping keep the animals healthy and safe. Kim smiled as she remembered her work with the big cats before becoming a criminal investigator. Once her twins were old enough, she would take them to the Zoo before it disappeared. Traditional zoos were falling out of favor, with people wanting to see animals in their natural habitats or wildlife parks.

After Kim sat for a few minutes, she had a craving for ice cream. Kim knew it would do her no good to ignore the desire as most of it was coming from the two lives in her body. So to the kitchen she went. A bowl of chocolate mousse ice cream helped satiate the twins' craving.

She watched the unblinking eye known as television as she finished her ice cream, then heaved herself off the sofa and towards her laptop computer. Hank found her a sizeable padded chair in place of the office desk chair. Kim soon surfed the various news sites to see if anything related to Homeland Security Investigations popped up. There were still problems at the Southern Border as people in Washington D.C. argued about 'border security.' That subject was above her pay grade, especially since she was on the Northern Border. There was a passing article on human trafficking and smuggling into Canada and Canada into the U.S. It wet her interest and made Kim wish her twins would soon decide it was time to enter the world. Kim loved the lives in her body but sorely missed her job. Luckily, she and Hank had enough funds stashed away to enable her to take unpaid leave off. Kim saved her regular vacation days and sick leave for real emergencies.

Then a short online news article caught her eye.

"David Roskin, confined in the Western State Hospital for the kidnapping and torture of reporter Rhoda Roberson, escaped from the confinement wing today. An all-points bulletin was broadcast to all law enforcement agencies. Roskin is considered dangerous and unstable. All Washington State residents are asked to share any possible information which may lead to his capture."

"Homeland Security Special Agents Richard Johnson and Kim Kupar were responsible for the original arrest of Roskin and rescue of Rhoda Roberson in a case which harkened back to the television series *The X-Files*—"

The internet article went on to talk about the bizarre and convoluted theories of Roskin and their connection with a particular investigative unit of the Homeland Security Investigation office in Seattle, Washington. Kim grimaced. Since going on maternity leave, Kim has isolated herself from the so-called Why Files weirdness. She hoped that she would be able to deal with more 'normal' investigations when she went back to work. As much as she enjoyed working with Richard Johnson and the others in the group, she saw enough weirdness to last a lifetime.

Kim leaned back in her stuffed chair and thought about Roskin. A complete nut job that the Virus had helped push over the edge. Kim had flattened him with an East Indian Martial Arts kick of which her instructor would have been proud. She was sure a person such as him would hold a grudge. Rex Moyer, the former training officer, had found a way with lead-free ammunition to qualify her just as Kim went on maternity leave, with some padding around her stomach to reduce the noise level for her unborn. Thus, she still had her service weapon handy.

"Just try something, asshole," she mumbled. "You'll be singing soprano."

Kim spent some more time surfing the Web but found no more details about Roskin. She glanced at the laptop's clock and saw it was just before Noon. Hank would not be home until after 5:00 PM, so Kim had another five hours to entertain herself. She'd tell Hank about Roskin when he arrived home.

Kim eventually put a DVD in the player of one of Senior Agent Richard Johnson's favorites. Her partner in the investigative group had turned her on to old Sci-Fi movies of the 1950s and 60s. The one she had chosen, *THEM!*, had special significance. Richard had experienced a classified updated version of the film. Kim smiled as she started watching the movie and thought about what it would be like if she went back to more normal investigations.

About a half-hour into the film, there was a knock at the front door. Kim pushed herself up from the padded sofa and did what she called 'her waddle' towards the main entrance. On the way, she picked up her service pistol. There was nothing wrong with being extra careful.

"Who is it?" she called out through the closed door.

"Rhoda Roberson. The investigative reporter you saved."

Kim cursed under her breath as she opened the front door a bit.

"Are you here because of Roskin?" Kim asked the tall brunette at her door.

"You heard too, yes? Can I come in? I am not acting as a reporter; I just have some information you might want."

Kim sighed. So much for peace and quiet until Hank came home.

"Okay, Ms. Roberson. I can offer you some coffee if you don't mind waiting while I shuffle around."

As Kim opened the door for entry, Rhoda looked at her large stomach. "Twins, right?"

"How'd you guess, Ms. Roberson?"

"Twins run in my family. I have seen many women carrying twins who had the same look as you."

Kim had Rhoda seated at the kitchen table as she brewed some coffee and placed some cookies and crackers on a plate.

"Please call me Rhoda, Agent Kupar. Ms. Roberson sounds so formal when I am not here as part of my journalistic professions, as some phrase it."

Kim smiled as she sat down. "Okay, then call me Kim. This meeting is off the record, right?"

"Right, Kim. I come here as a past victim of Roskin and do not want to see others victimized by that crazy piece of crap."

Kim handed Rhoda a cup of coffee and then sat down before speaking. As Rhoda added cream and sugar to her cup, Kim said, "You know something unique about Roskin."

Rhoda sighed, then answered, "The sick bastard has been sending me letters since his incarceration at Western State."

"Why didn't you block him?"

"Hell, I'm a reporter, an investigative journalist. I liked getting information from him for future articles, especially about how he and other patients are treated at Western State."

"Well, I guess you'll have a nice expose on the weakness in Western State security. A high-risk patient escaped."

Rhoda frowned as she spoke. "One of the last letters he wrote me, he hinted at having help from some patients rights group helping him with his release. I wonder now if the patients' rights angle was a cover for some other group to try and spring him."

"What type of group would do that? He was a sadistic nutjob; it all came out in court papers before a trial. Roskin was deemed mentally unfit to stand trial anytime soon."

"Ha! You, as a federal agent, should know, especially in the cases you worked, that there are a whole bunch of conspiracy people out there wearing tin foil hats. Some might even decide that to free a fellow conspiracy nut might just be the ticket."

"It would still take some doing, Rhoda."

"Ha! Western State is understaffed and falling apart. As I said, he rambled on about how crappy the place was once I got him going."

"Did he ever telephone you?"

"No way I'd give him my telephone number. And all his letters went to a P.O. Box so he would not know where I lived." Rhoda shivered a bit. "I still have bad memories of where he applied that stun gun."

"Well, stay safe, Rhoda. When you get the chance, forward me some of the letters, and I'll try to get some action out of my office. I may not be able to do much, but I can help light a fire—"

Someone knocked on the front door, then rang the doorbell. Kim and Rhoda looked at each other.

"Expecting anyone?" asked Rhoda.

"You were a surprise, remember? Wait here."

Kim recovered her service Glock and walked slowly to the front door as the occupants in her stomach began to kick once again. From the corner of her eye, she saw Rhoda pull a small revolver from her handbag. Kim hoped Rhoda had taken a good firearms course.

"Who is it?" Kim called out and wished she and Hank had invested in a doorbell camera system. It was always on the back burner of desired projects for some reason.

"Delivery for Kim Kupar, "answered a feminine voice.

"Leave it on the steps. I'm not dressed right now."

"I need a signature, ma'am."

Kim swore under her breath, then answered, "Please wait a minute."

The Special Agent stepped over and whispered to the investigative reporter, "I'm not expecting deliveries. Let me stall while I call the office for some backup —"

The backyard sliding glass door crashed into the recreation room.

"Call 911!" Kim yelled as she tried to move quickly without falling over towards the back of the house. She may be weighed down with twins in her stomach, but she could still shoot. Kim cut around a wall corner to find the threat when someone smashed in the front door. A shot sounded as Rhoda screamed in defiance, telling Kim the reporter had fired at a danger. Kim saw a cinder block sitting on the rec room carpet and realized it had been a diversion. Kim turned and tried to huff her way back to the front entranceway.

A large rubber bullet slammed into her right thigh, and Kim yelped as she fell. Kim managed to fall on her side to prevent injury to the twins in her stomach. She snapped off a shot at a dressed-in-black figure. A satisfying scream of pain told Kim she was still a good shot and that maybe the neighbors would call 911 after hearing the shots.

Then a Taser round hit her gun arm, and Kim screamed in pain.

Strange hands ripped the pistol from her hands.

"Keep fighting bitch, and your unborn may get hurt," a gruff male voice warned. Somehow Kim yanked the Taser prongs from her skin as she rolled onto her back.

"If my twins are hurt, I'll gut you all with a rusty knife — Roskin."

The wild-eyed and balding man loomed over Kim, and she saw he had the Glock aimed at her.

"You thought I was out of your life, didn't you, Scully?"

"This is not *The X-Files*, fool," Kim growled at the all too familiar face. A dark-clad man and woman dragged Rhoda towards where Kim lay. The Special Agent saw the reporter's mouth was bleeding.

"We need to move, people," said Roskin. "The gunshots will rouse the neighborhood. Karen, radio Jim to bring the van up to the garage." Roskin pulled some fur-covered handcuffs from an oversized pants pocket. "Look familiar?" the crazy man said with a leer on his face.

"You must have stock in some adult sex toy shop," Rhoda spat out.

"Hey, we could use zip-ties," the woman identified as Karen said while she pulled a radio from a small bag.

"Dave, keep a grip on Rhoda there," commanded Roskin. "She can be tough."

"I guess you don't care if we know who you all are," said Kim as she sat up.

"We're going for a quick ride. Then it's time for a live internet podcast about all the nasty secrets you all have. Once the truth is out about the Virus, the ZOG, the New World Order, our names will go down in history as true heroes."

Roskin was almost foaming at the mouth with

excitement. Kim saw all the time Roskin spent under psychiatric care had done nothing to improve Roskin's mental state.

"Jim won't answer," Karen said as Roskin bent over to place the handcuffs on Kim.

"Dave, zip tie Rhoda. Then go out and get Jim. He's probably listening to that Heavy Metal music at high volume again."

"Right, Boss. Okay, bitch, hold still while I—"

A large male figure lunged through the front doorway. A fist slammed into Karen's face, knocking her into Dave and Rhoda. Roskin straightened up and fumbled for the Glock in his waste band. Kim twisted and kicked him in the groin. Roskin's mouth formed an 'O' in pain a moment before Hank broke his jaw. Rhoda grabbed Dave and bit his face as she screamed like a banshee. Then Hank stepped over, ripped the man from Rhoda's grasp, lifted him like a rag doll, and piled him headfirst into the floor. Except for Hank's and the former hostages' breathing, silence descended on the house. Then Hank scooped Kim up in his massive arms and held her to his chest.

"You okay?"

"Now I am — Uh oh."

"What?"

"I think my water just broke."

Kim gave birth to a pair of very healthy Fraternal Twins in the hospital Emergency Room. The delivery was only a week and a half early. Kim's doctor said the two babies might have been born then, even without excitement and violence.

"Babies come out when they want to," Doctor Johansen said with a grin as he examined the twins. Then, minutes later, Kim was nursing her children. Hank stood by her with a huge beaming grin on his face. Kim looked at him with tears of joy.

"Why'd you come home early?" she asked.

"I thought I heard a tiger's cough even though I was in the office, away from the Big Cat Enclosure. Then I had this feeling…."

"Sir Kahn. He still protects the pride members."

Hank shrugged. "Who knows. It all worked out in the end. However, the cops told me I broke the guy named Dave's neck, Roskin's and Karen's jaws, and the guy in the van has a serious concussion."

"My loving husband. Hercules incarnate."

Hank Thomas bent over and kissed his wife. "No one screws with My Pride Members!"

Rhoda Roberson did an excellent write-up on the incident. "*Crazy Conspiracy Fanatics Suffer a Husbands Rage.*" The headline and story were soon flashed all over the various news outlets, and Rhoda was once again a frequent guess on the various talk shows and podcasts.

Roskin and his cohorts were all sent to maximum security correctional facilities. After all, attempting to kidnap a pregnant Federal Agent and a member of the Fourth Estate were not moves to gain new friends.

In between write-ups and interviews, Rhoda was

opening her letters and junk mail when she exclaimed, "Well, I'll be."

One of her fellow reports called out in the newsroom, "What's up?"

"I've been invited to a Christening by Kim and Hank." Rhoda soon had this massive grin on her face. "This old broad is going to be an Honorary Aunt!"

Somewhere in the many universes, a large hunting cat roared in approval.